I0764375

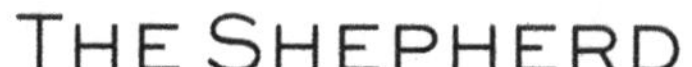

The Shepherd

The Shepherd

A Novel

Patrick Allen Mohn

Illustrations by Edward Carl Mohn

Santa Fe

Sunstone books may be purchased for educational, business, or sales promotional use.
For information please write: Special Markets Department, Sunstone Press,
P.O. Box 2321, Santa Fe, New Mexico 87504-2321.

eBook 978-1-61139-684-3

Library of Congress Cataloging-in-Publication Data

Names: Mohn, Patrick Allen, author. Edward Carl Mohn, illustrator.
Title: The shepherd : a novel / Patrick Allen Mohn.
Description: Santa Fe : Sunstone Press, [2022] | Audience: Ages 11. Audience: Grades 4-6. | Summary: While herding his father's sheep, Johnny meets a mysterious stranger in the mountain wilderness who provides him with two gifts--one helps him win "The Big Race," while the other allows him to bring about this story's miraculous conclusion.
Identifiers: LCCN 2022035073 | ISBN 9781632935793 (case) | ISBN 9781611396867 (epub)
Subjects: CYAC: Family life--Fiction. | Horse racing--Fiction. | Supernatural--Fiction | LCGFT: Novels.
Classification: LCC PZ7.1.M63827 Sh 2022 | DDC [Fic]--dc23/eng/20220812

LC record available at https://lccn.loc.gov/2022035073

WWW.SUNSTONEPRESS.COM
SUNSTONE PRESS / POST OFFICE BOX 2321 / SANTA FE, NM 87504-2321 /USA
(505) 988-4418

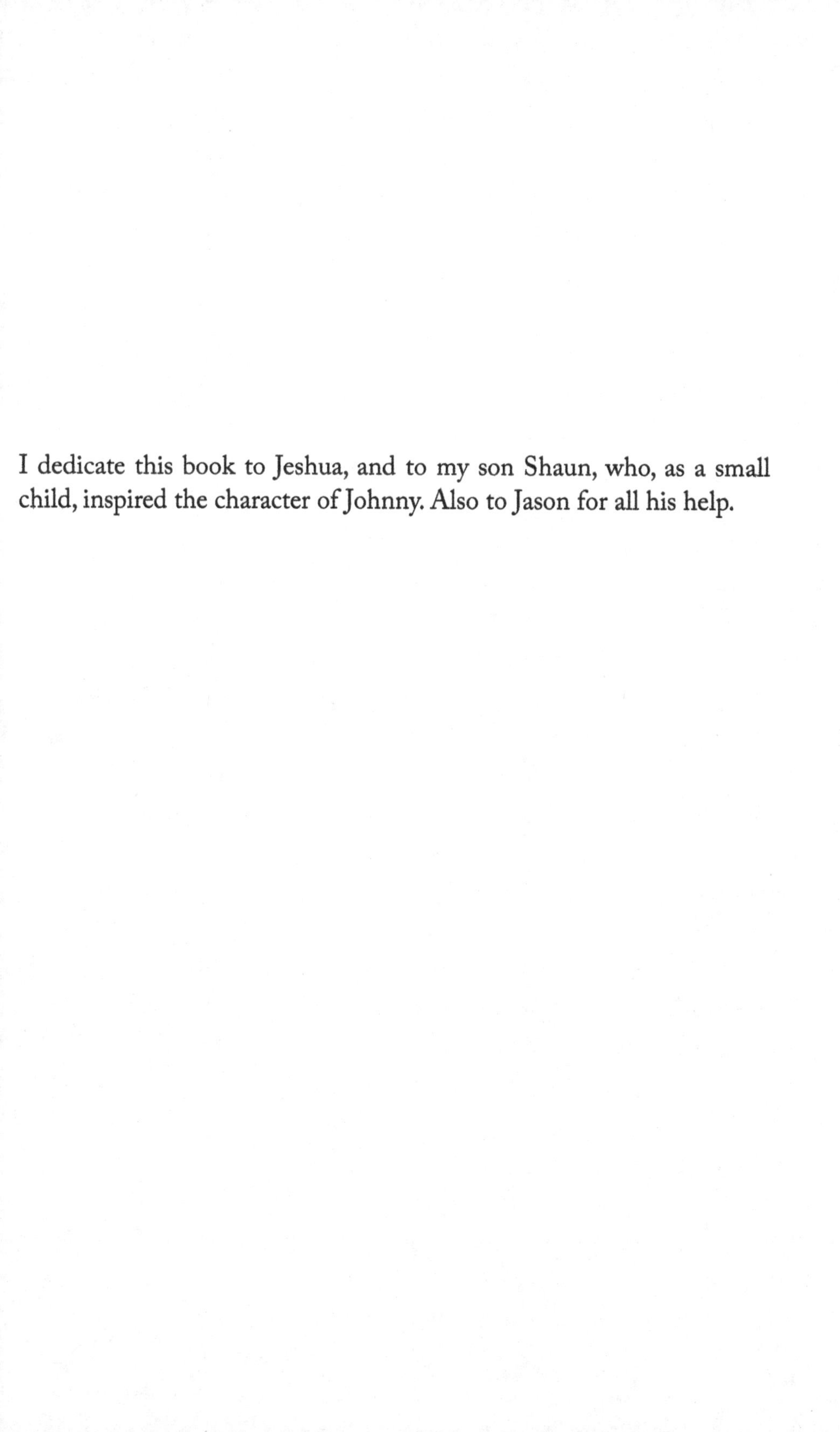

I dedicate this book to Jeshua, and to my son Shaun, who, as a small child, inspired the character of Johnny. Also to Jason for all his help.

Part I

A Friend in the Mountains

The Shepherd

Gray ribbons of mist rose from the earth. The slightest breeze whispered with the early light. The symphony of crickets and night birds found its end.

A manchild entered the stillness through the back door of his home. His hand let the screen door shut without a sound. Looking out at the cool morning, he felt it drawing him, and he walked into it.

He was small. Thick black hair covered his ears, framing a face of creamy skin, lightly tanned. His eyes were the color of the sky. He had on bluejeans tucked into brown shepherd boots and a hand made red, wool flannel shirt. A knapsack was slung over his shoulder. A long, sheathed knife hung from his belt.

As he sauntered through the backyard, he was joined by a Shetland dog.

"Hello Shep," the boy said. The dog jumped up at his face, licking him. The boy's laughter expanded into the gigantic volume of the mountain valley.

They walked on past the barn, the stable, then other buildings and sheds, to the last manmade structure: a high, wooden sheep pen.

The sheep could hear the rustling grass and their breathing as they approached. "Baah, baah, baah," they began bleating: first one, then more and more until there was a crescendo of excitement in the large but crowded pen. The boy swung open the long gate and soft, grey-white animals poured out, their pearl-white lambs jumping and skipping happily in freedom. He opened another gate to a smaller, adjoining pen, letting out goats of various colorations.

The boy with his dog herded the flocks up the valley. The dog trotted in, out, and around, forcing the individual creatures together as one organism. The child signaled him with slight movements of his hands and head. In this way, he controlled the exact direction of the herd, changing it at will. He did his work precociously, with perfect concentration. As one child might solve difficult mathematical problems, or another play artistically the piano, this one managed his animals.

The sun rose. Moist grass was bathed in sparkling, golden light. The boy was aware of the wet blades clinging to his boots as he pushed his feet through the pasture.

When they reached the top of the valley, they walked up a steep slope between two jagged pinnacles of rock. Soon they were deep into the wilderness.

After traveling a trail through thick forest that wound about rugged mountains, they came to a grassy peak and climbed it. Up went the grazing sea of creatures, rolling toward the top as waves, the sheep preferring grass, the goats nibbling bushes.

Eventually, the boy stood upon an outcrop of dark, gray-black granite at the summit. The clouds skidded past with wispy edges reaching, like fingers. The child jumped, trying to touch one, enjoying the sensation of warmth changing to very cool and back to warmth as it shielded him from the sun and then hurried on.

He took off his shirt and tied it around his waist by the sleeves. His little chest expanded with each breath of the high, fragrant atmosphere as he drank in and breathed out the teeming life that was everything, from the vast blue space to the rocks.

The air filled with little birds, darting swifts and bluebirds. And above as well as below soared the great birds; hawks, vultures, eagles. He could feel them watching him.

He moved his flocks onto a ridge. The child danced as he went, throwing up his arms in graceful circles. They descended for water into a broad valley. It had a small lake where elk stood, mirrored on the glassy surface.

Just before noon, they came to a high little valley perched upon the flanks of a tall, snow capped summit. Indigenous sheep were grazing along on cliffs above that reached into the snow. At the center of the valley stood a dwarf aspen tree by a spring. All around was a lush carpet of green grass. There was a ptarmigan nesting there.

"This is the place to stop for lunch Shep. Wha' da ya say?" and the dog "Yip! Yip!" yipped twice. So the child removed his knapsack as he sat down. Then the boy and his dog ate voraciously their enormous lunch.

~Shep~

When the feast was done, the child put on his shirt and laid back in the grass to watch the clouds go by through the foliage of the tree. He closed his eyes and listened to the gentle breeze, the birds' chattering and singing, and the munching of the sheep all around. Trusting them to Shep's care, he rested.

Whether he slept or not, the boy was not sure. But upon opening his eyes, he saw to his amazement a man standing nearby, looking down at him. He had not heard the man approach. He was tall, wore his jeans inside shepherd boots, like the child, but his shirt was white cotton. It was buttoned halfway up, and all the exposed part of his body was tanned. His skin contrasted with his long, snow-white hair and beard, falling thickly in shiny waves and ringlets over his shoulders and the upper part of his chest. His hair made him seem old, yet his complexion was young and waxy.

The boy wondered why he was not frightened. Instead, he felt particularly calm. At this moment was heard the triumphant melody of a solitaire. It was perched in the little aspen. Then the child realized that he was actually seeing his surroundings without looking at them, sensing them as through a dark mist with feelings coming from deep inside himself. All the sheep were lying down now, motionless. Their eyes appeared as lights, each pair fixed on this unusual person. Shep lay quietly beside the boy. He hadn't barked. The birds were completely silent. He could see all their little eyes, like sparkling gems, but without turning around. For the child was gazing at the deep blue eyes above him. And it was from those eyes that a profound calm was emanating, as if the whole world were being suspended in their spell. The man and the boy looked at one another for a long moment.

Finally, the man spoke, "You have come a long way, Johnny."

The boy glanced around and knew that he had never been to this place before.

"I have been watching you for a long time, waiting for you to come back to me."

"Have we met before sir?" Johnny asked.

The man smiled, "Let's go: I have something to show you." He began walking away.

Johnny got up and started to follow, Shep at his side. But then he stopped and turned to look at his sheep. They were still lying in the grass on the slopes of the little valley all around them. Three of the wild rams were watching from a rim of the valley close by.

"Don't worry about those sheep. They'll wait for you." The man tilted his head in the direction they had been going. "Come on," he said.

They walked up the grassy valley, then up and part way around the mountain. The way was steep, so Johnny had been looking down at the feet and legs walking before him. He noticed more and more patches of snow as they ascended. At one place, they had to walk through a drift deeper than the child's legs, so he stepped in the man's footsteps to get through. They stopped at last at a sunny spot. Johnny was breathing fast. He looked up then and was awestruck by what he saw. In the side of the mountain was a cave with snow clinging to the rocks above. A small fire flickered inside, near the entrance. Before the cave stood a roan stallion, nibbling on the sparse grass growing from the cracks in the rock. It was, by far, the most beautiful horse that the child had ever seen.

Immediately upon seeing them, he picked his head up from grazing and stared at the little boy.

"Is that your horse?" The child's voice was tenor and soft.

"No, it's yours," came the reply.

The stallion trotted up to him, snorting as he approached, wide-eyed. He nuzzled Johnny affectionately, almost knocking him down. Johnny was puzzled.

"Come on," the stranger said.

They all began walking toward the cave together, the man in front, the boy behind, horse and dog on either side of the boy.

They entered the cave and sat down behind the fire, facing out. Shep laid down in front of the fire. The roan horse stood motionless outside.

"Why is this happening?" Johnny inquired. He was looking out at some rocky cliffs. They were densely covered with squirrels, rock mice and chipmunks. It was a most unusual sight. They made not a sound and were looking right at him.

"Look at the fire," was the reply.

Johnny looked at the fire briefly, then back at the warm eyes questioningly.

"Keep looking", said his companion.

A great, tranquil feeling swept over the child. He looked quietly into the fire for a long time. His body felt like it was floating rather than sitting on the hard ground, and his eyes got transfixed on the dancing flames. His mind went blank.

After a while, he started seeing other colors in the flames. Suddenly they blended together to form a scene in the fire with people, and the people were his family: His father, his mother and his baby sister!

His father and mother were standing together looking down at their little daughter who was held by her mother. The baby was sick. Her limbs hung lifelessly. She was barely breathing. The parents' faces were haggard and old looking, riddled with anxiety. His mother began to cry.

For a long time, this scene remained unchanged and the boy watched. It seemed forever.

Then a light began to glow on them, freshening their skin. The pallor in the baby's complexion disappeared. Instead, she looked healthy. Her face came to life with a smile. Her eyes opened.

The dejected, fatigued faces of his parents brightened with enchantment and expectation. Their eyes, no longer dull and empty, grew moist and clear. Just when this wonderful change wrought by the light appeared complete, all three of them – man, woman, and child – together looked to the source of that light and a great transformation took place. Eyes were brilliant, shining lights, skin and facial features became animated, radiating fleshy color. Their expressions, even the babe's, were excited with ecstatic joy, raptured with utter happiness and love.

The sight of his family was so wonderful that Johnny was crying. He had gotten so involved in the vision that he was unaware of himself, and he was caught up in an experience of extreme emotion with his family.

Johnny was shocked back into self-consciousness when his eyes caught sight of his hands, which were luminous. He pulled back a sleeve and saw that his forearm, as far as he cared to uncover, was also brightly luminous. He looked back into the flames and realized that his mother, father and sister were looking into the face of the man sitting beside him, as if he were the source of the light upon them.

Very slowly the child turned his head, changing his view from the fire before him to the tall stranger at his side.

Johnny looked into his eyes. He couldn't stop gazing into them. Then the eyes expanded and the blue became a blue sky in a vision that contained many people sitting in the grass among bushes and trees in a lush green landscape, dotted with the beautiful colors of many wildflowers. There was a deep, blue lake before the people and somewhat below them. Behind the lake were bare, smooth-rocked mountains out of which flowed a high waterfall cascading down, down, and crashing majestically into the other side of the lake where the body of water hugged shear, bare cliffs of rock.

The air had a glittering, sparkling quality as if the light in the picture were almost a tangible, examinable object. In fact, the whole picture seemed to be made out of the bright daylight that illuminated it.

There were large birds with wings of tremendous length soaring in the shimmering air, the light glistening on their pinions as they performed graceful maneuvers.

All the people were looking up in the sky and to the right, beyond the scope of Johnny's view.

The loud whinny of a horse startled the child from his trance as his head snapped around to the entrance of the cave. The dished head of the roan looked in with innocent, inquisitive eyes just a few feet away. Johnny felt a great wave of affection for the mighty, yet delicate animal who was left out of the magical happenings within.

Johnny became aware of himself. He had again lost his self-consciousness, being absorbed in this second vision. He looked down at the fire, but could no longer see his family in the iridescent flames. He looked at his hands. They were still aglow, but now he could easily distinguish his fingers, which before were lost in the brightness.

"Why is this happening?" Johnny asked incredulously, shaking his head slowly, his mouth open, his eyes wide.

The man laughed heartily, pleased at the child's heightened interest. "You already asked that," he said. Can you think of something else you would like to know?"

"Who are you?" he asked.

An expression of utter seriousness formed on the man's face. "You already know me," he replied. "Let us just say that I am your good friend.

There was a moment of silence. Johnny felt happy.

"I am waiting for you to ask me a certain question," the man said, smiling.

The little boy was baffled at this, having no idea what he should ask. He felt confused, trying hard to think of what to say.

The man put his arm around the child. It was the first time he'd touched him. The boy felt a pleasant tingling spread down his shoulders and neck and up through his head. His face lit up as the wisdom reached his mind, coming from deep within. "What am I to do?" he asked confidently.

His friend smiled again and reached around a rock near them on the floor of the cave. From behind the rock he produced an instrument of a type Johnny had never seen before. It was a flute. But unlike other flutes made of wood or metal, this one was made, or appeared to be made, of glass.

After tapping it hard on the rock to show that it could not be easily broken, or perhaps for some other purpose, the man began to play the most wonderful melody that Johnny had ever heard. And as it emitted its rich, echoing music, the flute glowed brightly.

When the melody was ended, the flute stopped its glowing immediately. He handed the flute to Johnny, gesturing that he should try. But, though he tried in earnest, Johnny could not play a single note.

"I want you to learn to play this flute. You should practice each day while herding your sheep. But you may not show it to anyone until you are capable of playing what you have heard perfectly. You will not forget the piece. Having heard me play it, every part will remain forever in your memory.

"Here, I'll show you." With that he began instructing him, first in the proper technique of blowing. Then, after he could make a sound, Johnny was taught the various fingerings required to form the different notes. This took quite a while, but finally, giving his full attention to his tutor and his instrument, Johnny was capable of producing a variety of musical sounds and thoroughly understood the proper handling of the beautiful flute.

"You have learned well."

Once again, the two looked into each other's eyes for a long moment. Then the man got up and, smiling just a little, said softly, "You have to go now."

At this statement, Shep, who had been lying quietly all the while, was up, wagging his tail, panting with excitement. He moved quickly to Johnny's side. But the little boy was alarmed at the thought of leaving.

"No! Let me stay. Please, I don't want to go."

"What about your sheep?" his tall friend asked, laughing good-naturedly.

"Please. Let me stay with you. I don't want to leave," Johnny said.

"What about your family?" the man asked sincerely. The child had forgotten about them. It was a very close little family and, up until now, the other members of it had meant everything of real necessity to him. He bowed his head and looked down at the ground, scuffing the dirt with his foot. Then he looked up at the man and asked hopefully, "Can I come back and see you tomorrow?"

"No, but I will be watching you. And you will feel my presence. Believe me."

"Okay." Johnny looked down at the ground.

The man knelt down on his knees. He gently lifted the boy's chin until their eyes met.

"I will return to you again," he said. Then he hugged little Johnny and kissed him on the cheek.

Johnny was not sad anymore. "Goodbye," he said.

The man made no reply. He just smiled and they waved as Johnny walked away from the cave. With the flute in his hand, Shep at his side, and the beautiful steed following, the child started around the slope of the mountain. Then he stopped and turned.

"What's his name?" he asked, nodding toward the horse.

"You name him. He's yours."

When Johnny got to his sheep they all began to stand up. The wild, mountain sheep were all gone. Then the child and all his beasts walked home.

He practiced with his flute as they went. Birds kept with them, mountain jays calling mysteriously, wrens, canaries and bluebirds singing. The sheep baahed. The horse snorted and whinnied. And when Johnny played something shrill, Shep would howl.

Johnny felt wonderful. Though he couldn't coax the flute to glow at all, even when he played a correct note or two, just having the matchless

gift in his hands made him glow inside. And all the life around him was enjoying the same happy spirit.

There was a hollow tree containing a wild beehive not far up the slope from the valley of his home. The bees were friends to Johnny, who would often stop for a piece of honeycomb to chew in the mornings or evenings as he passed by. He placed the flute in the hollow tree that afternoon, thinking it would be a good place to keep it. Perhaps the bees were pleased with the idea because once the flute was inside, they swarmed suddenly, flying around the hive excitedly for several minutes. Then the whole swarm went back inside and became very quiet.

Johnny got a small piece of comb and walked on down the steep trail, between two jagged pinnacles, and into the high, grassy end of the big valley. This area served the sheep as a winter pasture whenever the snow was not too deep. From here he could see his father, way in the distance, working in one of his fields beyond the house.

'I will go to him,' he thought.

When they had made their way to the animal pens, Johnny put in his flocks and walked to the backyard. As he came through the gate he saw his mother standing in the doorway to the kitchen. She waved as Johnny and Shep came into view.

Sarah Watson Morgan was a beautiful young woman. She had the high cheekbones and round face of a Native American, with the fair coloration of a Scandinavian. Her wavy hair was parted on the side and hung past her shoulders. A big apron covered most of her cotton dress, but set off her full figure by pulling tight around her tiny waist.

Sarah loved her little boy.

Quiet and intelligent, he was always so willing to learn and do anything his parents set before him. Calmly, patiently, he went about his work, doing it very properly. But she often saw him standing somewhere, looking, as if he were hearing or seeing something not quite discernible to others, completely absorbed. Nevertheless, it was no small accomplishment that such a young boy could manage, single-handedly, his father's large and valuable flock of Rambouillets, as well as the little goat herd that tagged along. His appearance was striking: Shining black hair, delicately formed red lips, and big, azure-colored eyes with long black lashes made him a rare sight to behold. Her husband had been

very proud of his son from the moment of birth, a fact which especially pleased Sarah.

"Hi mom," Johnny called, beaming under her loving, dimpled smile.

Suddenly, she was taken aback as she saw a roan face peering shyly around the tall fence into the open gate. He seemed almost embarrassed as he looked into the unfamiliar yard. But after hesitating for a moment, he came trotting confidently up to Johnny, who turned to smile at his horse. He nuzzled the boy delicately on the cheek with his nose and snorted lightly.

"Johnny! Where did you find that horse? Who does he belong to?"

"Me," said Johnny

"Oh, honey! That's a very expensive horse. We can't afford to buy an animal like that!" She was noticeably disturbed by the unusualness of the circumstances, and also because she did not want her son to be hurt, knowing it would be impossible to keep the horse.

"I want to see my dad." Johnny was quite unaffected by his mother's sudden change of mood.

"Yes, you do that," she said. "And tell him to come wash up. Dinner is almost ready."

Johnny walked around the big log house his father had built when he and Sarah were just married. Johnny loved his home. He especially liked the stained glass windows with star-shaped panes that were high in the walls at either end of the high ceilinged parlour, and the big, stone fireplace that was also in the parlour. And he loved the yard which was a large area to the front, rear, and one side of the house. It was fenced with tall cedar posts, lined up to make a solid wall. All around the fence and the house were flowers and shrubs tended by his mother's hands. The front yard had a thick, green lawn arranged with rock gardens of flowers and beautiful stones, a spreading willow tree, and two peach trees. The back yard had big vegetable gardens on each side of the path leading from the gate to the back door, and a plumb tree. The side yard, through which Johnny walked now, was the largest and was a young orchard producing many kinds of fruit. The cherries were already ripe. There was a large strawberry patch, and against the long fence beyond the trees grew red raspberry, blackberry, and blueberry bushes. His father's beehives were located at various places in the side yard. All this did not

overwhelm the house which was tall and stately, built of rather massive logs. It had a high-pitched roof running from front to back. The house was simple in design, yet commanding in appearance. Johnny thought this must surely be the finest home in all the world.

He went through the front gate and down to where the valley broadened out. Here, before the house, were his father's great fields. Every year he added new ones with new kinds of crops to the virgin soil. Everything his father planted thrived. In years when other farmers had suffered from drought, insects or sudden storms, his father's fields still flourished. Here was a large field of melons, here oats, here wheat turning gold, there was the big barley field in the distance, down below. And at the far side of the valley, near the stream, was the green alfalfa. 'Perhaps it's the high altitude,' Johnny thought. 'Perhaps that's why Dad's fields always look so nice.'

As he reached a field of timothy, Johnny turned right, walking between wheat and hay to the end of the little road where his father was bent down working among the beans. Johnny walked between the bean rows with Shep beside him. The stallion stayed close behind.

Jacob Morgan was so intent upon his work that he didn't hear them coming. He failed even to notice the sound of light stepping hooves in the soft soil of his new bean field.

"Mom says to come wash up for dinner," Johnny said softly.

His father turned and looked up, smiling, pleasantly surprised, the sweat pouring down his brow. But slowly, through the haze of his exhaustion, a look of shock formed on his face as he recognized the silhouette of a horse's head beyond that of his son above him. He stood up, now towering over the boy. The man was shirtless, in overalls. His arms and torso, nearly black from exposure to the sun, rippled with muscles. His handsome and very dark featured face appeared to get much darker as he set himself to verbally chasten the child for bringing a horse into his bean field.

He opened his mouth but was halted in his speech before any sound came when it dawned on him that he had never seen this horse before. Indeed, this was, he thought, the most beautiful horse he'd ever seen.

Jacob walked over to the side of the well-behaved animal, standing quietly between the rows, and began a careful examination of the equines

conformation with his eyes and hands. He went all the way from front to back and down the legs, while the immaculate roan remained perfectly still. He then turned to face his smiling boy with a stern look.

"Where did you get this horse?"

"In the mountains."

"This is a valuable animal. It's a purebred Arabian stallion. Someone will be looking for him." Jacob looked down compassionately at his boy. "He does seem to like you, following you around all this way. But, son....

"Let's go up to the house. We'll discuss this after dinner."

Jacob walked with his son, his hand resting on the boy's neck. Occasionally he looked back at the roan's face directly behind Johnny, and each time he shook his head in disbelief.

When they got to the house, Jacob told his son to put the horse in the old paddock on the side of the house. "Give him a sheet of that real blue alfalfa from the lower part of the field, a couple sheets of timothy, a bucket of oats and some water," he added, then went on into the house.

Johnny was very happy with this choice of quarters because the old paddock was right below his bedroom window. It contained a three-sided shelter, one side of which was a wall of the house. The open side faced out, away from the house. There was a manger and water trough inside. His father had built the paddock while building their home. He had only one horse then. Now Jacob possessed several teams and had long ago built a nice stable. Sometimes he spoke of taking down the old paddock and its accessories to use the lumber for something else, but had never gotten around to it.

After providing the food and water Johnny put a wooden box beside his new horse, stood upon it, and began brushing him until he gleamed in the afternoon sun. He finally stopped after his mother called.

Dinner was the beginning of the evening which was the time of reward and togetherness for the family.

His father was already seated, the table already set when Johnny loped in and took his chair.

"Where's the princess?" demanded Jacob loudly and gaily. In came little Emily bourn in Sarah's arms. "Yes, there she is!" cheered Jacob and Johnny as her mother set her in the highchair next to Johnny, who had the honorary job of helping her eat.

"There," Sarah exclaimed after tying on a bib. The baby smiled.

Her big green eyes looked at everyone as she turned her head all the way around in a big sweeping motion, losing her balance but for the chair which held her securely. Then strange unknown words emerged very clearly from her little red mouth.

Jacob gave his customary word of thanks for the food from the Lord's bounty.

There were lots of talking and laughing during dinner, mostly concerning Emily and her attempts to feed herself through every pore of her face. They all laughed uproariously at times when their center of attention did something particularly funny, and at Johnny when some of his attempts to help her ended in disaster.

After dinner, Jacob, Johnny and Sarah together cleaned the table and washed the dishes. Then everyone bathed. At last, they retired to the parlour.

It was a large room, taking up fully one-half the inside space of the house. It had a tall ceiling with beams in the pitch exposed. High up at each end of the room were the stained glass windows. Beneath one of these was a picture window looking out into the backyard. Under the other one was the front door. It was made of oak, very thick with attractive patterns chiseled into it. The door was held in place by long, forged hinges of iron. To the left of the door was a staircase leading upstairs to the bedrooms which were built over the kitchen, pantry and washroom. These rooms, taken together, composed the other side or pitch of the house. Down the middle was a balcony traversing the central length of the house, serving the bedroom doors. Under the balcony was the dining area with its long oaken table. Jacob built the large table, he said, to help feed the big family they would have someday.

All four reclined together facing the fireplace. Johnny, in his pajamas, sat between his parents. Sarah held the baby.

"All right, son, tell us how you came to be in possession of that horse," Jacob said.

He began at the beginning, telling all the unusual incidents of the day. His parents listened quietly. When he finished, there was an audible silence that lasted for a long, tense moment. Johnny looked at his mother, who was looking down at the baby girl, frowning. He looked up at his father and found two black eyes glaring at him, set in a very dark, drawn up, irritated looking face.

"Do you really expect us to believe a crazy story like that?" Jacob said. "Is this the kind of stuff that goes on in your quiet little head?" His voice was not harsh. He was genuinely intrigued by the mysterious child. He couldn't help wondering just what kind of kid they were raising.

"Listen to me. In a few weeks we are going down to the village. I have to look for someone trustworthy that I can hire as a permanent hand around here. While we are there, I will ask around discretely of certain people and find out who owns the horse so that it can be returned. Don't count on the idea that we won't find him. Someone is sure to be missing a horse like that. And we'll hear no more of these fairy tales. Are you trying to upset your mother?"

"No sir." For the first time in all this long day, Johnny felt gloomy, partly because he was stung by his father's words. But there was more. Jacob's reaction to his story disturbed him. 'He can't believe what I saw,' Johnny thought. 'He can't believe what I saw.'

Feeling for Johnny's predicament, Sarah changed the subject of conversation. "When did you decide to hire someone? I am so glad. This place is too much work for you all by yourself. You need help all the time, not just at harvests and at the sheep shearing."

"I've been thinking about it for a while," Jacob answered, "but I guess I finally decided to do it just tonight. Actually, though, the reason I'm doing it is that I want to add some new crops next spring and I might as well go ahead and break someone in on the place now. He can help at the harvest, help me plow this fall, and this winter he can help me feed and care for the stock since Johnny will be gone to school.

Here was something else Johnny was not happy about and tried not to think about at all. He was to start school this year, in October, and would have to stay with relatives all week. He could only come home on weekends when the weather was good. But he put aside this subject and went back to his musings. He thought back to the days when his dad first took him out to trail the sheep. "This is where a man should spend his life," he would say, "up here with God."

The flock was smaller then, and they didn't trail them up very high. Johnny made such a good shepherd that Jacob started letting him go out alone.

His father changed after that.

"But Jacob, don't you have enough crops? What good is it going to

do us to have you wear yourself out? There's more than enough. You can't keep pushing yourself like this. I'd like to see more of you."

"Darling, I have the land and the strength. I can build this place into something that our children can have. Besides, this soil is so good. Everything I plant grows up strong and yields huge harvests. Its like magic."

Johnny looked at Emily lying on her mother's lap. She seemed restless and pale. She sneezed. Then she started coughing. Sarah picked her up, laid her on her shoulder and patted her back gently.

"May I be excused?" Johnny asked. "I want to go to bed."

"Its kind of early...all right, son, go ahead. Kiss your mommy."

Johnny got up, kissed his mother, then kissed his little sister very tenderly. "Good night," he said.

His parents watched him as he walked wearily across the parlor, up the stairs, and onto the balcony to his room. He closed the door behind him.

"Poor little guy," Jacob said. "He must really want that horse to make up some crazy story like that. He's pretty sad."

Sarah placed Emily, now asleep, beside her on the couch and looked up at her husband.

"Jacob, he's always been such an honest boy. Let's forget all about this tale of his and not bring it up anymore, not even between us. Maybe he'll get over the horse. In a while, we can get him a nice pony to ride, he's old enough."

Jacob Morgan gazed lovingly at his wife. He reached out, holding her cheeks in his palms. What a wonderful companion he had in life. She was wise and sensitive and she was gorgeous. Sarah hadn't aged a day in seven years. Her red blond hair had a bright sheen like some precious, polished metal. Yet, it was so soft to touch. Her complexion was as creamy and smooth as ever, not a wrinkle or line. And her bright green eyes: He knew that he was entrapped by them, submerged in a warm, mysterious sea. They laughed at him.

"What?" she asked innocently as he smiled.

"You know what," he said.

She snuggled into him, curling up under his brawny arm. She drew her legs in under the nightgown so that her bare feet rested on the cushion.

Yes, he worked like a slave for this woman and her children, and no wonder.

Johnny laid in his bed, but wasn't tired. Now he wished he'd never seen the vision of Emily dying. What could he do? He could show his parents the flute. They could explain away the horse, but how could they explain a flute made of glass that didn't break. No, he had promised. He couldn't show it to anyone, not yet, and probably not for a long time. But what could he do?

"I know," he said to himself aloud. He would go back to the cave tomorrow and ask his friend. 'Surely he won't get mad if I go to see him just this once,' he thought. 'He'll help me. He'll know how worried I am.'

Johnny felt better. He knew what to do. Everything would be fine.

Now what could he think about. 'Ah! A name for my horse. Let's see...' He thought of all kinds of names and thought and thought. He fell asleep with the name on his lips.

Johnny got up real early, while it was still dark. He got dressed and went out onto the balcony. As he passed his parents' room Sarah called to him through the open door. "Why are you up so early, Johnny?" She was sitting on her bed, nursing Emily.

"I want to get an early start today."

"But I haven't made breakfast yet," she said.

"I'll grab a bite on my way out."

"Oh dear," she said and sighed. She was not looking forward to having breakfast without her son.

Outside, on his way, Johnny crossed paths with his father, carrying milk buckets to the morning milking.

"Where are you off to?" Jacob asked.

"I want to get into the mountains."

"But, what about breakfast?"

"I already ate," Johnny said. He had a determined look in his eyes.

Jacob thought of restraining him at first, but decided against it considering what had happened the night before. 'Maybe he needs a little time to be alone,' he thought.

"Go ahead then, but try to be home earlier today. Four or five hours is plenty of grazing for those sheep. You don't need to keep them out so long as you do."

"Yes sir," Johnny said, and was gone. First he went to the far side of the house to let his horse out of the paddock. Shep was there, too. He had apparently spent the night.

"I guess you two are pals, eh?" He gave Shep the scraps he'd brought for him from the pantry. Then he poured some oats for the horse and brushed him until they were eaten up.

"Come on," he said, walking out of the paddock, leaving the gate open. He went quickly to the big sheep pen. Shep was beside him, but the satiny roan kept licking the manger, trying to get the last scattered oat grains. Then, suddenly, he wheeled around and came flying out of the shelter, out of the paddock at a fast gallop, and across the open field to Johnny, bucking and kicking out with his hind legs into the cool, moist air of the early dawn.

Johnny opened the gate of the sheep pen. It was a big, solid plank gate and the rest of the pen was a solid wall of planks too. It protected the sheep from predators and, as a windbreak, served as the only shelter for most of the flock from the cold of winter.

Out trotted the sheep. Quickly, through the pasture, heading away from the log house, then up the steep trail between the pinnacles they went. When he reached the hollow tree and had pulled out the glass flute, Johnny turned around to look at the burning, golden red clouds hanging over the valley, which had high mountain walls draped with thick, primeval forest of Engelmann spruce to the north and south, an opening to the east, and a deep saddle to the west behind the rock pinnacles.

They continued up the slopes. Johnny was driving the sheep faster than usual and did not take time to practice his flute. He had but one thought: He must find the cave and re-enter the wonderful bliss he'd found in the company of his new friend.

Soon the child and the animals found themselves lit from behind in golden light. Their feet were all wet from the heavy dew in the grass. The horse nibbled the bushes as he walked by them and frequently stopped to munch on some green grass. He would lag behind a ways, then trot up to the boy and walk with him.

Johnny herded his flock across a ridge and down into a narrow gorge. In one place the walls were so sheer that tree roots grew horizontally out from under overhanging boulders, with the tree trunks bending around

the boulders until they could straighten vertically and shoot skyward. The bottom of the canyon had a little stream with thick patches of grass growing in spots on either side of it. He recalled having come this way, but when the canyon split, Johnny couldn't remember which fork he'd taken. He had not really watched where he was going the day before. Johnny was familiar with these mountains and had never become lost, but he often wondered joyously through them only half aware of where he was going. He finally decided on the smaller left fork and was sure that he was right when he reached a high waterfall a little further on. It was unmistakable. Beside it, about halfway up, could be seen a nest of young water ouzels behind a rainbow in the misty spray of the falls. The parent birds were gliding along the cascading, bending watercourse below, and landing on boulders to sing, and their music mingled with that of the rushing waters.

Johnny and Shep drove the sheep up the steep, rocky sides of the canyon, around the waterfall. The horse watched until everyone was out of the way. Then he ascended, too, galloping up the near vertical climb at a tremendous speed. It looked impossible. The child could not prevent himself from laughing. He could see how much easier it was for the animal to come up this way rather than one step at a time, but it was very funny just the same. He went up to the panting horse, got onto a big rock and leaned on him, hanging one hand from his withers.

"You looked like a sky rocket," the boy told him.

Above the waterfall the rough canyon became a roundish valley with an emerald bottom and a saddle at its end. Johnny let the sheep graze a little here, then they went up on the saddle and crossed a rock-strewn avalanche lane to a long, high spur carpeted with alpine flowers where colorfully painted butterflies and hummingbirds fluttered and darted about. The ridge afforded Johnny an extraordinary view in every direction. Both sides disappeared suddenly down into deep, narrow gorges cut into solid rock. The peaks of very high mountains stood before him and somewhat to his right.

To Johnny the mountain peaks seemed very close, like friends standing near to him in a conversation. The ridge was joined to one of these peaks up ahead. To his left and right, stretching out into the distance, were canyons and ridges, making straight, then curving lines around some more mountains behind him. Beyond the canyons were

endless ranges of rugged mountains: rock and crystalline snow. They gleamed in the morning sun, every detail sharp in the eyes of the keen sighted child through the thin, clear atmosphere.

As he started walking the flocks toward the peaks, the boy became confused. Johnny had been feeling a great elation when he had reached the top of the ridge the day before. Then, as now, he had walked toward the white summit before him, the spur curving gently up and into it. After that, in his memory there was only the recollection of entering into the little valley. When he was leaving the valley, a feeling of great exuberance had filled the child as he joyfully played his flute.

'How did I get to and from the little valley?' he wondered.

He spent the rest of the morning and much of the afternoon looking among the high peaks, but he could not find the cave or the little valley with the lone aspen tree in the bottom.

Finally, in mid-afternoon, Johnny gave up his search and, after taking a long, careful head count of the sheep and goats, he headed dejectedly toward home.

In a while, he decided to practice the flute as he walked along. 'Its the only thing I can do,' he thought.

Though his playing was not of the finest quality, it did attract the various species of birds in the area. A camp jay landed on his shoulder, then another landed on his other shoulder. These were replaced by others as the large, friendly grey and white birds took turns riding on either side of Johnny's head. Soon birds were all around; white-throated sparrows singing happily, and the hermit thrush with its marvelous, melancholy song, traveling right along with the herd. Marmots whistled shrilly, close by and high overhead, from their rock-strewn homes. The sheep had eaten their fill by this time, and everyone was marching home over the mountains, down from the alpine meadows and into the cathedral like trees of the forest where light came down in bright streams, to the tune of Johnny's unskilled playing.

Gradually, Johnny's spirit rose. And by the time he got home late in the day, the boy was in a much happier mood than when he'd left early that morning. He found his whole family standing in the warm, yellow sunshine near the sheep pen, watching for him. They were all moved at the sight of the child's coming. Emily reached out her arms for him to take her and hugged him, digging her little fingers into his shoulders.

Johnny spent most of the evening holding her. They fell asleep together between mom and dad.

From then on, Johnny practiced his flute every day when he herded his flock. His progress was slow. Still, he could see that, gradually, he was getting better at playing it. And he could always remember the intricate melody his friend had played for him. It had been so beautiful that Johnny could not forget it.

He often looked for the cave too, whenever he took the sheep to that part of the mountains.

The child kept good feelings with his parents after that. Yet, he remained apprehensive about Emily, though he never mentioned it. It was not only the vision that caused this. There were many evenings when she would again have a coughing spasm unexpectedly, and sneeze, then appear listless and pale. It would usually occur on evenings when their father would come in from his fields overly tired. With increasing frequency he came to the house in a state of utter exhaustion.

Yellow Marmot

Part II

The Big Race

"Nobody works today," Jacob said, as Johnny walked into the kitchen. "Today we are going to town."

"Oh boy!" Johnny was almost gone before Jacob could stop him.

"Wait a minute. Where are you going?"

"To harness the team," he answered excitedly. He hadn't been down to the little village in over three months.

"You are still small to harness the team, son. Besides, we are not taking the team. We are taking just one horse and the buggy this time. We don't have to buy many supplies or take anything to market. The buggy will be faster and lots more fun."

The child was beaming.

"Johnny, you know I'm going to look for the owner of your friend. I hope that doesn't put a damper on your good mood."

"No, sir," Johnny replied smartly, and his full smile broadened further.

Jacob and Sarah looked at each other uncomprehendingly.

"Well, wait for me to finish my pancakes, Here, have a glass of juice. Sarah, better bring this boy a big stack."

After breakfast, Jacob and Johnny went out and harnessed Jacob's best horse, a long-legged, black mare with a white star on her forehead, to the family buggy. Then they went to the old paddock where Jacob attempted to halter the roan. But when the noseband came in contact with his face, the horse instantly bolted backward. Then he snorted loudly between careful sniffs of his widely flaring nostrils, his eyes open big and round.

"From the way he acts around you, I'd have thought sure he'd at least be halter broke. Well, something's going to have to be done. He's pretty big to be without any training, and a stallion to boot. He could become a nuisance.

"Let's leave him here for today." Jacob went on. "I'm just going to talk to a few close friends of mine who know the horse world hereabouts. I'll be discreet. But I'll find out who he belongs to."

The buggy ride down to the village that morning was a happy affair for everyone. Sometimes they sang songs. Sometimes they just looked at the scenery. Shep came along, running beside the buggy.

As they descended their valley, it soon got steep, the land untillable. Gradually it became a deep, wide gorge thickly forested with spruce and aspen. There were big boulders of granite piled against each other all around in the canyon bottom. Ferns grew here and there among the rocks in the dense shade. The little stream got bigger and bigger as they continued. The gorge terminated at a fork after several miles, where it opened onto a much larger canyon. The sides of this one were very high with sheer cliffs at their tops, and it was very wide, filled with ponderosa pine and Douglas spruce. Down the center of it flowed a gushing river which was flanked with aspens and blue spruce.

Here the trail made a sharp left, crossed through the stream, then followed the river. Mostly, it took them high above the water where often they had breath-taking views of the cascading, swirling torrent.

Not long after entering the big canyon, they stopped to rest the mare for a few minutes at a small meadow next to a place on the river where it slowed and formed a big, gray pool. The morning sun filtered down through the trees onto green grass and colorful little wildflowers.

Johnny jumped out of the buggy and stretched. Then he and Shep crossed the meadow and climbed to the top of a large boulder next to the pool. Slowly, two heads peered over the rock to watch the wary cutthroat trout, who were casually swimming about in the still, clear, icy cold water. Across the pool, two beavers were hard at work, sitting on their tails and cutting some willows. Jacob and Sarah sat down on the grass and leaned on the giant trunk of a pine. They played with Emily and talked.

Soon the family was on its way again, traveling down the majestic canyon for nearly an hour before it began to widen into a broad, fertile valley. They passed farms and ranches for several miles. The aspens along the river gave way to the narrow-leafed cottonwood. They saw the sawmill way off to the left, then the fairgrounds to the right. After another space of open country, they began encountering the little wood houses on the edge of the village. Jacob finally stopped the buggy in front of the residence of Jeremy and Ruth Conway. Ruth was Sarah's older sister.

Before climbing down, Jacob opened his wallet, took out twenty dollars, and handed to Johnny. It was Jacob's custom to pay his son for his work as his shepherd whenever they came to town.

As the family descended the buggy, the seven Conway children shot out of the house running toward Johnny, yelling excitedly. There were four boys and three girls ranging in age from three to twelve. Jeremy and Ruth waved from the porch. The man was blond and smiling, and possessing, as Johnny recalled, an almost constant good humor. Sarah's sister was dark, favoring the Apache of their ancestry. Her long black hair was pulled back in a chignon.

Johnny went to the backyard to play. All four adults and Emily went into the house and sat down at the kitchen table for coffee. Emily got homemade raspberry jam on buttered toast.

The kitchen was small, having bright yellow wallpaper and white curtains with little yellow flower prints. The ceiling, window panes and door frames were painted white. There was a sink and an icebox against one wall and a yellow enamel wood cookstove next to the window on the back wall. Opposite the icebox and sink were long, white shelves holding packages of food, a set of copper canisters, and perhaps two hundred filled canning jars. Iron pots, pans and cooking utensils hung near the stove and on either side of the doorway to the parlour. In the center of the room stood the wooden table and chairs on a wooden floor. Flowering yellow begonias overfilled the sills on both windows.

"It's been a long time since we've seen ya. We were startin' to wonder if you were all right," Jeremy said.

"Do you know, we haven't had one major problem since we moved up there," Jacob responded after reflecting a moment. "Your family seems to be a healthy outfit."

"Yeah, we're doin' pretty good. I got a raise at the mill. I'm next in line to be foreman. I envy you though, buddy, bein' out in the sunshine all day up there in the high country."

There was a pause, and then Ruth said, spontaneously, "Hey, Sar, Jeremy's been investing money in some stocks and making real good." Ruth's personality had a reserved, quiet mien, curiously mixed with occasional moments of impetuousness.

"Oh, Ruthie, that's wonderful," Sarah was genuinely happy for them, knowing how much the profits would help in raising the children.

"Why don't you invest in some stocks?" Jeremy asked Jacob. "The market's really a' climbin'."

"You know I don't play around with money more than I have to. I like the land and the soil."

"Maybe so, but I still think it's somethin' that a college guy has turned farmer and don't even bother with a bank account," Jeremy said.

"Ah, I majored in agriculture, remember? And, anyway, we've got our own bank, a little treasure box. We put all our money in there. It never runs out. Usually there's a lot in it," Jacob said. He thought a moment, rapping his fingers on the table top. Then he added, "Jeremy, here's a hundred... nah, here's two hundred. Why don't you invest it for me. Keep fifteen percent of the profits for your trouble. What da ya say?"

Jacob held out the money. Jeremy swept it up with one hand while sticking out the other. The two men shook on it. "Partners," they both said together and laughed.

There was a quiet moment; everyone sipped their coffee. Emily smashed toast against her mouth, smearing jam across most of her face.

"We really worried about you," Ruth said seriously, caringly. "Jeremy and Amarante were getting ready to ride up there.

"Do you worry about the kids, Sar, bein' way up there so far from a doctor?"

"No. I used to worry about Johnny, out herding the animals all alone. I was worried constantly. It was the only thing wrong with living up there. Otherwise, it was heaven."

"What happened?" Ruth asked,

"I had a dream."

"A dream?" It was obvious from the expression on Jacob's face that

everything Sarah had been saying was completely new to him. "When," he asked pensively?

"It was over a year ago."

"What did you dream?" Jeremy asked, intrigued.

"I dreamed that I went up in the mountains looking for Johnny. I was calling out his name. Then I came to a place I used to go when I was just a little girl. I had completely forgotten about that place." Sarah looked at everyone. Seeing their interest, she settled herself. Calmly, she went on.

"It was a very little valley, set up high an' lovely on the other side of a snow-capped peak. It had cliffs on three sides going down and a cliff on the fourth side, too, from the inside of the valley, going up the mountain. But there was an easy way into it. I used to go there when I was sheep-herding with Gramps, whenever the sheep camp was on that side. I liked to go up there and sit by myself for a while. I was just seven an' eight then... Anyway, in the dream, I was there again. I sat there in some sedges by a little spring where it joins the mountain until all the animals and birds came out and started playing, like I used to do. I had the same marvelous feeling, as if I was in the safest place in the universe. It was so wonderful to be a little girl again. I started to cry.

"Then I heard music, rich and beautiful. I felt it coming out of my soul. I was looking all around, but then I lowered my eyes to a draw where this little waterfall flowed out of the valley. You can look down through it to a deep canyon, and there I saw Johnny, herding his animals. Between me and him, beside the waterfall, was a cougar and a grizzly lying down together on the ledge. They were watching Johnny and looked like they were smiling, like he was making them so happy that they could be pals whenever he was around. I woke up then, still crying, with the music still in my mind. Now, after that dream, I just always know he's safe."

"Why haven't you told me anything?" Jacob asked.

"I knew I would," Sarah answered, "when the time came."

There was a long silence. Then Jacob said, "I worry about him, a lot.

"I only meant for him to trail the flock to those crags standing in the pass, spend a little time there, and come home, like we used to do together.

"But I've gone out on horseback to look for him because he's got

to staying out too long. I've never been able to track him down. But I see where they've been. He wanders his flocks all over. They go above the timberline. I've found their sign in some of the craziest places. He takes those animals to terrain you wouldn't think any sheep would ever go. Once, I actually gave up and turned around to find myself looking down on some wild mountain goats!

"I've been telling him to cut it out, but I know he still does it because he's always gone all day. I have thought and thought, trying to find a way to put an end to it, but I can't."

"Why not?" Jeremy asked, incredulously.

"He's built that herd up more than four times the size it was when he started herding by himself. And I haven't even been trying to do that. I've sold quite a few sheep.

"He never looses any. All the ewes lamb. A lot of them have triplets and they all live. They all get big, too. They're aren't any runts. The herd is strong. Those ramboullets are the most valuable asset we've got, by far, in spite of all the hard work I put into that farm. The only reason for it is that Johnny is a topnotch sheepherder. You can't argue with success like that."

Jacob stood up. It was time for him to leave. He had business to take care of.

"First, I want to go to the stock yards, then I need to visit some friends.." He hoped to hire someone suitable as a year-round hand.

Ruth, Sarah and Emily were going shopping. Each woman took her white gloves, parasol, and hat. Sarah wore a red cape dress, while Ruth's dress was green with bell sleeves. They walked slowly, ever so gracefully, down the sidewalk, pushing Emily ahead of them in a stroller. The warm summer air was alive with a light breeze that played gently with the material of the women's dresses.

Jeremy wanted to stay home. It was his day off from work, and he planned to relax. Everyone was to meet back at the house at two o'clock.

Johnny played with his cousins for over an hour. Then he and Tommy went for a walk downtown. The other kids all went into the house to munch on the fruit Jacob and Sarah brought as a gift. There were three bushel baskets; one was full of cherries, one had apricots, the other contained blackberries. Everyone stayed around the house

with their father, waiting, knowing what to expect when the two boys returned.

Johnny especially liked Tommy, who was a quiet, polite boy of five years. He had been born with one leg shorter than the other and walked with a limp. His father worked at the sawmill and made a good living for the family. But having so many children, he wasn't able to provide them with many extras. So the first place the two went was into the candy store. After buying a good stock of sweets, they went down the street and turned into the drugstore. At all the other stores Shep waited patiently outside, but at the little black-tiled Rexall he went right in with the boys who sat at the counter and ordered root beer floats. Then they ordered seconds.

The next stop was a clothing store where Tommy donned a new green and white cowboy shirt with pearl snaps for buttons. Right next door was the dime store. Johnny bought every child a toy, a game for the whole family, and bags of warm peanuts and cashews. Johnny gave some money to Tommy and let him pay.

On their way home the children passed MacGurdy's Bootery. Johnny liked to stop and look at all the fine boots in the window. One pair immediately caught his eye. It was a pair of real cavalry boots made for a little boy. They were knee high, crafted of polished brown leather with a strap that buckled across each instep and another that buckled across the top of each boot on the outside of the calf. Johnny looked at them carefully, then walked into the store and right up to Mister MacGurdy, who was not busy at the moment. He was a tall man with gray hair and long sideburns. His smile revealed large, gleaming white teeth.

"Well, howdy boys. Why, Johnny Morgan, haven't seen you in a coon's age. What can I do for you young uns'?"

"Could I see that pair of boots in the window, please?" Johnny asked.

Dale MacGurdy picked the boots out of the window and set them next to Johnny's feet, scratching his chin. "These are real expensive boots. They were handmade for a boy whose father ordered 'em and never returned to pick them up," remarked Mister MacGurdy.

"How much?" Johnny asked.

"Well, all together, twelve dollars and fifteen cents."

Johnny pulled out all the money he had left and counted. There were exactly twelve dollars and fifteen cents!

"Do you think they will fit me?"

"Well, lets just find out." Tommy watched as Mister MacGurdy put the right boot on Johnny's foot. It fit perfectly. He had Johnny walk around a little to make sure it was comfortable. A big smile broke across Johnny's face.

"I'd like to wear them," he said.

Mister MacGurdy put Johnny's shepherd boots into a box while Johnny put on the other cavalry boot. He paid the twelve dollars and fifteen cents, received a receipt and the shoebox and thanked Mister. MacGurdy. Then the boys and the dog headed for Tommy's house.

When they arrived, Johnny found his father standing in the yard talking to a man he had never met before. Tommy went straight into the house carrying the candy, toys, and nuts, and wearing his new shirt.

"Johnny," said Jacob, happy to see his son, "I'd like you to meet an old friend of mine. Matt, this is my son Johnny. Johnny, Matt Slade."

Matt smiled at Johnny in a way that made him feel noticed. He reached out his hand to the boy. "Pleased to meet you," Matt said in a tone he might have used to another grownup.

Johnny took his hand. He liked Matt right off. He was a man of about forty five, not so tall as Jacob, and thin but wiry, with a strong grip. The wrinkles in his tanned face formed round, friendly lines, and his light brown eyes sparkled. He had long, shiny brown hair that covered his ears, all except the lobes, and disappeared into his shirt collar in back. A black cowboy hat hung on his back by a drawstring. A large, red bandana was tied around his neck.

"How do you do, Mister Slade."

"You just call me Matt."

"Matt is coming with us," broke in Jacob. "I've just hired him as my new hand."

Johnny looked at Matt and smiled.

"Your father tells me you're the owner of a very fine horse."

The boy turned to his father questioningly.

"Well," Jacob said," Matt says he's never even seen a horse like the one I described, much less heard of one lost. Everyone else said about the same thing."

“I’m looking forward to meetin’ your friend,” said Matt.

“Matt has spent most of his life as a horse trainer,” Jacob explained, then added, “I guess that horse is yours, Johnny, until such time as someone else comes along that can prove otherwise. Why don’t you think of a name for him?”

“I already have. His name is Joshua.”

Both men chuckled. “Real nice name,” said Matt. “I like it.”

“Yeah, me too,” said Jacob and then, pointing to Johnny’s new boots, “Hey, what’s this?”

Johnny felt embarrassed. He had never spent so much money on himself at one time before. Most of his money he just saved at home. Then, at Christmas time, he’d buy everyone real nice presents, at birthdays too. “Well,” he said, “I saw them in the window and liked them. They fit perfect and I had just enough money left to buy them....” He was at a loss for words.

“Fine,” said Jacob. “They look real nice on you. Good quality I’d say.”

“Yes,” added Matt. He bent down on one knee for a closer look and touched them, examining them closely. “Very serviceable riding boots. Excellent. Where did you find them in your size?”

“At MacGurdy’s,” replied Johnny. Then he noticed that Matt wore a very similar kind of boot. And he no longer felt embarrassed.

“I’m going to pack up my things, Jake,” Matt said, standing up. “I won’t be long”

“Okay, but no hurry. We’ll be visiting here for a couple of hours.”

The two men shook hands.

“See you later Johnny.”

“Bye, Matt,” Johnny replied as the man walked away.

When Matt returned both families were on the front porch, the adults sitting in chairs, the children playing with their new toys. Johnny and Tommy were playing marbles in the yard. Shep was asleep on the grass.

Matt was riding a very tall mare and leading another mare with a packsaddle containing his belongings. The two boys in the yard walked up to Matt. Johnny could tell what the pack mare was, a quarter horse with a beautiful chestnut color, bald-faced with four white stockings.

Her coat shined brightly like a new copper penny. But he didn't know what kind of horse Matt was riding.

"Hi Matt," everyone called. Matt waved.

Johnny stroked the shoulder of Matt's tall mount. "What do you call her color?" he asked.

"It's called a blue roan," Matt replied. "She's a Thoroughbred," he added, sensing Johnny's wonderment at her proportions.

"Where'd did you come by such fine horses?" Jeremy asked as he and Jacob walked up from the porch with Jeremy's other three sons.

"Well, Jennifer there I've had for many years. She was my only horse for a long time. This one's name is Dianna." He stroked the neck and shoulder of his temperamental mount, smiling at her.

"I got her at the last place I worked. She was only four months old when I bought her. They weaned and sold off their colts there real young. She was a beautiful baby, an' real frisky. I had never raised a colt myself and decided to buy the little filly. That was four years ago. She was expensive but worth it. I've never been sorry.

"Shall I climb down for a while?" Matt asked.

"No, let's get going. We're all packed up and ready, too.

"Jeremy." Jacob said, turning. He shook hands with his brother-in-law, "We'll be seeing you."

"Okay," Jeremy replied. Then, reaching up to shake hands with the other man, "Hope you like it up there , Matt," he added.

"I think that place is just right for me. Take care of yourself, Jeremy."

Everyone said their goodbyes, and Jacob and his family, with Matt, began their journey home.

Johnny thought Matt looked really splendid sitting on his tall, lean horse with the other horse behind, all packed up. Once out of town, Matt invited Johnny to ride with him. Johnny climbed up behind him on the big mare. It was a new experience for Johnny. Not only was she very tall, but she was alert, quick, and confident. She had confidence in herself, and she had confidence in Matt. Just riding there behind Matt, feeling the movement, Johnny learned how to ride a horse. He didn't even have to try to learn. It just happened.

When they got home, the men began unloading the buggy.

"There's room for you upstairs," Jacob said to Matt.

"Naw, Jake. You got a room somewhere away from the house? I'd rather have it that way, if its all right."

"Sure. You can have the tack room out in the stable. Its got room enough for some furniture. But you will be having your meals with us, won't you?"

"I sure will do that."

Johnny went with Matt to help him move into the tack room. He watched carefully as Matt took down his packsaddle, seeing how it had all been put together.

"Let's take a look at your horse," Matt said after getting his own ready for the night.

"Come on!" Johnny was anxious to show him.

They walked around the side of the house where their eyes were filled with splendor as the red, afternoon sun lit Joshua up for them.

"That's the reddest, red roan coat I've ever seen," Matt remarked admiringly.

They went into the paddock, and Matt examined Joshua all over. "Your father was right," he said finally. "He's about as fine an example of an Arabian horse as could exist, except he's so tall. He has long legs, almost like a thoroughbred. But he's an Arab, there's no mistaking it.

"Johnny, you're a real mature boy for yer age," Matt began after a pause. "Your father tells me you have some crazy story as to how you came by this horse. I'd like to hear your story, that is, if you don't mind to tell it."

Johnny hesitated, frowning. But then he looked up at Matt and decided that telling him the story would be a good idea. He recounted everything to Matt as he had to his parents. There was a long pause after Johnny finished the story. "It's okay if you don't believe me."

Matt looked squarely into Johnny's eyes. "I do believe you," he said.

Johnny smiled. He put some oats in Joshua's manger and began brushing him. He felt strangely pleasant inside.

"You know, I have a story, too, and I've never told it to anyone. Would you like to hear it?"

"Sure," Johnny answered.

"Well, when I was a little boy like you, I lived on a farm, kind of like you do. My dad had this old workhorse he'd put out to pasture because he was old. I used to ride him around the pasture. 'Go ahead,' dad would say. 'It's good for him.'

"Me and that horse got to be good friends over the years. I got him to where he'd do all kinds of tricks, and we used to put on a show for the family sometimes, and sometimes the neighbors too. His name was Oak.

"Then, one day, when I was twelve, we found Oak out in the pasture. He had died. I was real broken up. So the next day, dad went out and got me a job on a big horse ranch nearby. It was owned by a friend of his and I was to be apprenticed as a trainer. I wasn't interested at all, but Dad said, 'You do this for ol' Oak, son.' So I did. Before long I was the best trainer on the place.

"The owner had a pretty little girl named Rachael. She used to watch me working the horses. We never talked much, but over the years as we were growing up, we came to be in love. When we were old enough, we got married. I bought us a little house out in the woods and painted it in bright colors. It was red, yellow and blue with a white picket fence all around the yard. She planted flower gardens everywhere, and in between there was a thick lawn of blue grass.

"We were real happy. We wanted kids, but she never had any. She felt bad about that, but I told her, 'We'll adopt some, give them a good home.' I meant it too. We were going to do just that.

"Meanwhile, I was making quite a name for myself as a horse trainer. I was ambitious. I wanted to quit working for people and start raising and training my own horses. I was real happy, on top of the world.

"Rachael used to read the Good Book. She went to church every Sunday, and I'd go with her because I liked just to be with her. She wasn't very social in the church, but she'd read the Good Book every evening.

" 'I feel so close to God, Matt,' she'd say. 'I want you to feel it too.'

" 'I do,' I'd say, 'just being with you.' But that wasn't what she meant, and it used to bother her.

"Then one day she said, 'Matt, what if something were to happen to one of us?'

" 'Why, don't talk like that, Rachael,' I said. 'We'll still be together when we're old and gray.'

" 'But...what about after that?' she asked. "Wouldn't you want us to be together after that?'

"She had a point. I didn't want anything to ever separate us. It bothered me for a long time. I even picked up her Book once and tried to read it. But I couldn't make any sense out of it.

"That winter was unusually severe. The snow piled up so high we even had to dig out around the windows. It got so cold that no matter how much wood I burned, the house would not get warm.

"Every winter Rachael would get bronchitis. But I would stay right with her when she was sick. I'd take care of her and do things to cheer her up and she'd always get better. But that winter, she got sick and stayed that way for months. The constant coughing and her congestion kept making her weaker. Then, towards the middle of January, a blizzard hit and it got colder than any time I could remember in my life. The wind blew day and night, and the house was cold inside. I kept her in bed right by the stove. But it didn't help. She got pneumonia and died.

"That was the end of my life as far as I was concerned. I didn't go back to work the next spring. I just stayed home and kept all her flowers real nice and the house just the way it was. I dusted and cleaned around her things so they remained right where she'd put them last. I didn't think much. There wasn't anything to think about.

"One very beautiful summer day, I was working out around her flowers when I heard her call my name. I wasn't thinking about anything at the time, I remember that. My mind was completely clear. Maybe I hadn't had a thought in my mind for hours or days. I don't know. But I guess you could say that at that moment, I had forgotten she'd died. So when I heard her call me, I turned around. I didn't see her and couldn't figure out what was going on, and then it was like I could almost see her. All of a sudden I remembered she had died and yet, at the same instant, I realized she was right there with me. I smiled. I smiled because I was glad that she knew that I knew that she was still there, loving me. Then I felt real weak and cold. My body was shaking all over, and I was barely able to get into the house and lay down. I started crying. It wasn't that I was happy or sad. I was pure emotion. That's all there was. Maybe that's how a baby feels when it's first born. I kept crying for hours and hours. Long after it was pitch dark, I was still crying. Then I fell asleep.

"I woke up when the gray light of dawn was first filtering into the house. I walked outside and watched the sunrise.

"I decided to give away everything except for some clothes for me

to wear. But when I was going through Rachael's things, I came across her Book and saw a marker in it with 'Matt' written on it. I opened it and found a place she'd underlined. It said, 'I'm going away, but I will return to you again.'

"Well, I kept reading. Now all of it made sense. I kept that book. It was the only thing of her's that I kept. It's right over there in the tack room with my gear. I read it every evening like she did."

They watched the brilliant, fiery red sunset. The whole sky was ablaze. Matt, Johnny, Joshua and Shep were all aglow with its light and their moist eyes sparkled red.

"That's exactly what my friend said to me," Johnny remembered. 'I will return to you again.'

Johnny and Matt were both smiling now. Then a gloomy look came over Johnny's face. "But those things I saw really bother me. Especially Emily getting sick. And mom and dad don't believe me at all. All dad cares about is working this place.

"Do you know what those things mean that I saw?" Johnny asked suddenly, hopefully.

"I know what the second vision was, the one you saw in your friend's eyes. That's the place we're all goin', all of us who live in the Spirit. After all the bad things are over, we'll all be there together. There won't be any bad then, and we'll all live for ever. Even death will be gone."

"What about what I saw in the fire?"

"I don't know what to tell you about that. It was for you and your family. But it's good you're concerned. You have to help yer family come into the Spirit. Don't get worried, though, you will. You're in the Spirit and you'll help them. It'll just happen."

"What is the Spirit?" Johnny asked.

"That's what you felt when you were around your friend. It's Life. Spirit is what makes us live. It isn't really the food, and money doesn't have a thing to do with it. You've got the Spirit, Johnny. Help others to find it. That's your job."

"How will I know what to do?"

"You'll know what to do. The Spirit will show you."

There was a pause. Johnny wasn't convinced.

"There's a place in my Book that says this world is like a ranch

where the owner went away for a long trip and left the whole spread in the care of the workers. After a while, some of those workers started taking advantage of the others. They got real mean.

"Did your dad ever tell you about the war?"

"Nah, he never talks about it. Mom told me that dad was in it though, that he was a hero."

"Yes, he was," Matt said. "He saved his whole squad. It's quite a story. But Jake doesn't want to think about the war. It was bad."

"Were you there?" asked Johnny

"Well, I was in the Army. But they mostly sent the younger guys over to France. They put me to work training cavalry mounts. I never left the States.

"But, look, lots of people think everything is all right now. They're making big money in the cities. They think that's all that counts. But there's a drought out on the plains and in the Midwest. It's been dry for several years. In any other industry, a product shortage would force prices up. But agricultural prices have stayed low. The whole economy has gotta hold of the farmers by their throats. My book shows me that harder times are coming on this Earth than anyone has ever seen before. You'll have to grow up and face those times, Johnny. When you get big, remember yer friend and what's happened to you. When things get real bad, the Spirit will help you."

It was still scarlet down on the horizon, but mostly the sky was now shades of purple and lavender. There was nothing more to say, it seemed. But Johnny was still worried about Emily and his parents and what he, a small boy, could possibly do to alleviate their suffering should it come. His anxiety showed in his face.

"Your dad says this horse hasn't had a bit of schoolin'," Matt said. "Why don't you and I start training him tomorrow?"

"What do we do?" Johnny asked, curiously.

"First, we've got to halter break him. Here, I'll tell you what. Get that halter over there and put your box under his head and stand on it."

Johnny did what he was told.

"Now, let him sniff the halter."

Johnny slowly raised the halter to Joshua's nose. At first the horse snorted loudly and acted very suspicious of the odd-looking contraption.

But he didn't back away, and after a while, he relaxed and even started nibbling on the halter with his lips.

"Now, slip it on and clip it together."

Johnny did it, and Joshua didn't mind at all.

"Yep. He likes you real good. He trusts you. I'll tell you what, there's a big race the seventh of October down at the fair. I helped set up the first race years ago. It's a good cross-country race of twelve miles. Lots of horses are entered every year. But you might win with this horse. If his training goes along as good as I think it's gonna, why don't you enter?"

The child's eyes got big, and a strange tingling went all through him. He had never even ridden a horse by himself before.

"Do you really think I could?" Johnny asked, hardly imagining it could be true.

"Sure!"

"Hey, you guys, come on in here and eat!" It was Jacob calling from the back door.

"We're coming," they both yelled back together.

The next day Matt began working the farm with Jacob, and in the evening, he helped Johnny train his horse to lead. A few days later, Joshua was performing all his gaits obediently on the lunge line, so Matt began lunging him with Johnny up. Now, for the first time, the child was riding his horse.

Matt wanted him to learn to ride bareback first. So, for many days, he rode bareback around and around in the training area. He learned to sit straight at the walk, bounce evenly at the trot, and use his knees at the canter. When Johnny had developed a good seat, it was time to put the saddle on.

"Why don't I teach you to ride English," Matt suggested.

"What's that?" asked Johnny.

"Its like cavalry riding. In fact, I've got an old cavalry saddle you can have. It's a nice saddle, light weight, forward seat, and it has places to tie things on for a long horseback trip. It's a great all-purpose saddle."

Johnny liked his new saddle. It went well with his cavalry boots. It was a little big for him, but it fit Joshua's back perfectly.

Then Matt began driving Joshua fully tacked up, saddle and bridle. Every evening they worked, training Joshua carefully, one step at a time. Joshua trusted Johnny and Matt and enjoyed his lessons. Everything went smoothly. In about one month, Johnny was riding the horse by himself, and the horse was not only well schooled in all the basic elements of riding, but had a smart way of going as well.

"Now we'll start conditioning for the race," Matt said. "I'm going down to the village tomorrow on business and I'll enter you while I'm there."

That evening after dinner Matt discussed the idea of Johnny's entering the annual cross-country race at the fair with Jacob and Sarah. Jacob, knowing Matt's fine judgement as a horseman and trusting him completely as a friend, was very willing. But Sarah was apprehensive.

"What if Johnny falls off and even gets trampled by the other horses?" she asked. It was obvious that she was completely opposed to the idea.

"There's always an element of danger in a race like this," Matt explained. "I wouldn't suggest Johnny enter his horse and ride him, except that he's already a better horseman than many adults and his mount is intelligent and sensitive. I believe the horse would protect Johnny even if he did get into trouble, which is unlikely. There are no jumps. Its just a cross-country run and we've got two months to get ready.

"There is the element of danger. I'd be lying if I said there wasn't. But it's not a big risk. Johnny is a very mature boy for his age. I think he needs a man-size challenge right now. He wants to do it, and I personally feel that it would be the right thing to let him."

Sarah looked at her son sitting calmly at the table across from her. He was a little boy. But his spirit was not a little boy's spirit, nor was it a man's. He had all the qualities of a child that made being a child wonderful. He was happy, spontaneous, innocent and fresh. But there was also something else about Johnny, something different. Sarah looked into his shining blue eyes, so tranquil, so deep, so clear.

"All right, angel. You go ahead and race your horse. I want you to."

"Well, I'm going to give you a run for your money," Matt said the next afternoon when he returned from the village. "I entered you and

Joshua, and I entered me and Dianna too. So now we'll be conditioning together real early in the morning before the sun is up, then again in the evening before dinner. We'll take it pretty easy at first, gradually building them up."

And so at dawn, Johnny, Joshua, Matt, Dianna and Shep were out cantering in the early mists.

Johnny was very hungry at breakfast that morning. He thought that food had never tasted so good. Then he went off into the wilderness with his flocks. Jacob and Matt worked in the fields and around the farm. Sarah took care of Emily, the house and the yard. In the evening, Johnny and Matt rode together again. This routine went on for several weeks. At dinner, everyone came together. Matt was like a new member of the family. Emily was still the center of attention. She was learning to feed herself better and received lots of praise for her progress.

After dinner, Matt usually retired to his own little room in the stable. But, occasionally, he ventured into the parlour with the family for just a little while. When he did, he always took the baby and entertained her. Matt had a special knack for making her smile and laugh. Emily took to Matt naturally and kept calling him by name. "Maah," she would say, pointing at him. "Maah," sounding like a goat kid. Everyone laughed.

And Emily quit coughing, much to Johnny's relief. He felt better about his family now.

'It's Matt,' he thought. Matt did add to the baby's happiness, it was true, and only infrequently did Jacob come in from the fields thoroughly spent. He worked as hard as ever, but was so excited over all that was being accomplished with Matt's help that it overcame his exhaustion. The man was already figuring out where he was going to cultivate new ground and what he was going to plant there next spring.

Johnny witnessed day by day the quaking aspen change their dress from emerald green to brilliant, shimmering gold streaked with red; a solid bank of foliage, rustling with every breath of breeze along the stream across the verdant valley from his bedroom window.

Camp Jay in Aspen Tree

By mid-September the higher mountains were clogged with snow and Johnny wasn't allowed to herd his sheep anymore. The very last time he went out, a strange thing happened. He was trailing the sheep up a little valley in mid-morning when he noticed a wolf lying on a flat rock above him, not more than twenty feet away. It kept staring at him. But none of the animals appeared to notice, not even Shep. As Johnny moved his flock along the gurgling, sparking creek, the wolf moved too, staying close above the boy on the slopes. He was large and had a thick winter coat, almost pure white. He looked very much like a dog except for his slanting green eyes and sloping tail. Johnny was frightened at first, but then he felt the wolf to be smiling in a friendly way and the child became accustomed to his company, even enjoying it.

Meanwhile, the sheep and goats grazed on up the valley, bleating serenely to one another, as if unaware of the predator's close proximity. The air was cold and crisp that day at those altitudes, filled with the aroma of autumn mingled with the scent of snow that drifted down from the snowfields. The wind blew occasionally and, when it did, Johnny could see the wolf's coat spread back easily in the breeze, revealing the downy fineness of his fur.

In the afternoon, as he started the flocks toward home, the boy heard a howling in the distance. Johnny turned to look for the wolf, but he was gone.

After that, the sheep were let into the big pasture formed by the upper end of the valley above his house, stable, barn and animal pens for a small part of each day. The horses, cows, and goats were turned out with them. In a few hours, they were all put back into their stalls, paddocks and pens and fed hay.

Now Johnny had different things to do. He worked with his father and Matt harvesting the fields. He helped his mother, mostly by taking care of Emily while Sarah went about doing her chores. Also, he rode. He took Joshua and Shep upon the mountain sides that flanked the valley and farm like walls.

"Just walk 'em," Matt cautioned "If you run him all the time, you'll spoil him and pretty soon that's all he'll want to do. Besides, he gets all the running he needs mornings and evenings. You don't want to wear him out. So just walk 'em a lot and that'll be a good thing."

Joshua's hooves struck comfortably on the soft, humus-covered slopes. Johnny stopped often to look down at his home from one viewpoint and then another. At times he watched his father and Matt working way down below. Or he'd see his mother set Emily down in the bright autumn sun and water the fruit trees with a bucket from the hand pump in the yard. Sometimes he could hear their voices carrying up through the high, crystalline air. Always he carried his flute with him on these rides, but retreated behind a crag or into a ravine in order to practice so that no one could hear.

Finally it was October. The harvest was just about in and the week long fair had begun. The buckboards were filled with farm produce to be taken down for sale. Some outstanding examples were entered in various competitions and so were Jacob's best rams. Many of the lambs were taken down for sale. Sarah's cherry pie won first prize that year, a great distinction, and one of Jacobs rams ended up with a blue ribbon.

Everyday both of Jacob's buckboards were hitched up and loaded. Jacob drove one with Sarah and Emily at his side. Matt drove the other, and Johnny and Shep rode with him.

Then, on the last day of the fair, the day of the race, Jacob took Emily and Sarah down in a buggy while Johnny and Matt rode their horses alongside. A heavy frost coated that morning. The air was crisp. The trees and the forest floor were white. All three horses stepped high and nickered to one another. They were obviously excited, feeling strong.

Matt was wearing his calvary uniform. Johnny wore a pair of real riding breeches tucked into his calvary boots, a fancy red shirt that his mother had made for him, and a bright green kerchief around his neck. He was confident on his big stallion.

During the past few months, he had developed a closeness of relationship with Joshua that was different from any other he had known. He and the horse were as one creature. This is what Johnny felt: The powerful animal beneath him responding to his every signal, signals that were given spontaneously. The two were bent on accomplishing the same purpose, whatever it might be. They were soully knitted together.

When they pulled up to the Conway house, Matt told Johnny to come with him. "I'm going to take you and Joshua around the course first thing," he said. "There'll be officials all along the route during the race, and anyone getting off the course will be disqualified."

The course began at the west end of Main Street. There was a big sign overhanging the street that said "START", and long, red ribbons floated in the breeze tied to gas lamps on either side of the cobbled thoroughfare.

"You'll see those ribbons all along the way," Matt explained. "You have to stay between them. They mark the course."

Asking their mounts to walk, the horsemen rode down Main Street through the center of town. Then they turned right, or south, down a residential street until they came to the river at the edge of the village. They turned right again, going upriver toward the west until they could see the fairgrounds in the distance with its many tents and pavilions, colorful pennants streaming from their pinnacles. The sounds of the crowds traveled electrically to them along with a clear, twinkling vision of the people and much activity. Now they turned left and crossed the river over a wooden bridge to emerge into the shady solitude of the pines where they began following various trails.

The horses got very frisky in the cool dampness of the forest and kept trying to break into a run. But Matt insisted they hold them back in a walk. Actually, the compromised gait they went at was a kind of collected, prancing walk.

Johnny enjoyed riding with Matt on their big horses through the dense forest. The trails kept changing, and there were a lot of turns and curves, but the red ribbons made it easy to tell where to go.

They meandered in an easterly direction until they rode into the open again far downstream from the village.

The sagebrush was higher than the horses' bellies, a bright, glistening blue in the sunlight, with a strip in the center of feathery yellow and lavender-purple blooms; the rabbit brush and wild asters near the river banks.

"What kinds of trees are those?" Johnny was pointing to the mountainsides flanking the valley below them. The short roundish trees growing there did not shade the ground, and the rocky hills looked hot and dry in the windless sunshine. The air smelled dusty and unfamiliar.

"Those are pinon and juniper trees," Matt told him.

It was the first time in his life that Johnny had seen them. At that moment he knew, somehow and for certain, that he would someday

leave the sanctuary of the high mountains, which had held everything that he had ever known.

The pair crossed the river in a big bosque of giant, broadleaf cottonwoods, canopied in dazzling yellow, then headed north across open fields and irrigated farmland until, plunging into more of the dense, fragrant Ponderosa forest, they took the winding trails up the other side of the valley.

On and on rode the horsemen, passing the village somewhere along the way, eventually coming out of the forest three-quarters of a mile above the fairgrounds. From here, they turned straight toward the fair and passed right through the center of it where people were walking in every possible direction. Finally, the course crossed a small field and into a grove of very tall, bright, red-leafed maples. About two hundred feet down the colorful, leaf strewn lane that went through the grove, they came to a stop under a large sign that said "FINISH".

The ride had taken over two hours, and it was after ten o'clock. They rode back to the Conways', and here Matt suggested they rest their horses until a quarter to four when they should begin leading them casually for an hour to loosen them up, while making their way to the starting line. The race was scheduled for five o'clock sharp.

"I promised Tommy I'd take him for a ride," said Johnny in his self-assured and untroubled manner.

"Okay," Matt replied, "but have Joshua back here before noon so he can rest up."

The first place the boys rode was to Mister MacGurdy's bootery. "You hold Joshua for me, Tommy. I'll be back in a few minutes."

Tommy was a sandy-haired boy with a patch of freckles across his nose. He was just the kind of kid you'd think would be all over the place and into everything and indeed he was as a toddler. But when he got old enough to be aware of his handicap, he mellowed rather suddenly. Now, he mostly walked instead of ran and did not frolic so much with other children.

In a few minutes, Johnny came back outside. "Come on in," he said to Tommy, and tied Joshua to the hitching post.

As they came in the door, Dale MacGurdy looked down at Tommy,

a stern expression on his face. Tommy peered shyly up at the tall, gray-haired man.

"I'd like to take some measurements of you," said Mister MacGurdy. "Is that all right?"

"Ah-huh," replied Tommy.

So Mister MacGurdy took measurements of Tommy's legs and feet. Then the boys said good-bye and went outside.

Johnny helped Tommy up on Joshua's back, then climbed up himself. They rode through town and out into the country, through the woods for quite a ways.

"You're lucky you get to go out in the high mountains by yourself. I wish I could do that." There was sadness in Tommy's voice.

"Hey, you can Tommy! Tommy's face brightened at Johnny's excitement. "You can come with me!"

"Aw, I'd just slow you down."

"No you wouldn't. I don't have to walk anymore. I got Joshua to ride now. We can both ride him, just like we're doing!"

"But he'd prob'ly get tired, riding us both all day long.."

"Nah, Joshua never gets tired, no matter what."

They were quiet for a while.

"Most of the kids don't like me to go places with them. But I don't care. I like to be alone," Tommy said.

"Me too," Johnny replied. "But I'd like it if you came with me. I could show you my favorite places. Maybe we could even find my good friend. You'd really like him."

"What good friend?" asked Tommy.

"The one who gave me Joshua."

There was a pause.

"We'll ask your mom and dad if you can come stay with us next summer. Then me and you can go trail the sheep every day."

Tommy smiled. It was the first time Johnny had ever noticed a sparkle in his friend's eyes.

Lastly, they rode into the fairgrounds. They found Carol and Linda, two of Tommy's sisters, and got them to buy them each some cotton candy and popcorn and then some soda pop so that the boys wouldn't have to dismount.

When they'd seen everything at the fair that could be seen from

horseback, they rode to Tommy's house where Joshua was unsaddled and rubbed down, especially his legs, with Tommy's help.

That afternoon about 3 p.m., Matt and Johnny met at the Conways' and began brushing their horses. Then the horses were bridled, saddled and led for nearly an hour in a round about course to the west end of Main Street. There, the officials began lining up the entries behind the starting line. There were sixty-three official starters, making this a much larger field of racers than ever before. They were lined up nine abreast and seven deep. Johnny was put in the third row; Matt was back in the fifth. Johnny was the only rider under twelve years of age. Many eyes looked at him apprehensively. The horses were agitated, and Joshua was extremely so. He pawed the road impatiently, putting his head down. He screamed wildly in a low pitched, guttural voice. Sometimes he would move forward and to one side or the other, but Johnny would check him easily, bringing him back into line.

People were saying things like, "How did this little kid get into the middle of this mess?" But there was no way now to stop what was about to happen.

The gun went off and there was a mad rush of horses charging down Main Street. Hundreds of people packed in on either side were yelling and cheering. The horses were all fast, high-spirited, and grained up; horses that liked to run, the pampered favorites of their owners, prepared all year for this one particular race. Matt had told Johnny to hold Joshua back at first to conserve energy for the many miles ahead, but Johnny couldn't bring himself to rein his horse in. In the turbulence of this violent, thundering sea of horsehide and hooves, Joshua had gotten off so fast that Johnny had to hold his main with both hands just to stay in the saddle. They made their way so swiftly through the pack that before reaching the turn at the end of Main Street, Joshua and Johnny were leading by more than a length. Then down the streets of the village, they increased their lead. Galloping across the wooden bridge, they were far ahead of everyone. But after entering the cool and quiet forest, Joshua began to slow down. He slowed almost to an easy canter. Then horses began to approach from behind and he picked up a little, but only a little.

As other racers began passing them through the winding trails in the pines, Johnny did not try to push Joshua to run faster. The boy's

exhilaration at the start of the race had been all consuming. He was satisfied. He patted Joshua on the neck and spoke softly into the stallion's ear. "You've already won the race for me," he said.

Soon Matt was coming up.

"Let 'em go at his own pace," he yelled to Johnny as he went by.

Twenty, perhaps thirty horses back, Johnny finally settled into a stable position in the lengthening stream of horses and riders. There was a buckskin in front of him, and a big, dark bay just to the rear. They stayed in this configuration for a long while. No more horses passed by and none to the front dropped back.

Then the racers broke into the open, each in his turn. Now the bay was moving up. Joshua didn't appear to notice until the bay's head was at his flanks.

They were traveling under the big cottonwoods by the river. Suddenly, as if awakened from a trance, the red and white stallion looked back at the bay and snorted. The child could see Joshua's right eye gleaming fiercely. He lengthened his stride and speeded up, neighing loudly, the noise coming out with each exhale of his powerful lungs. He took the buckskin and then, crossing the open fields, passed other horses. One by one, he and Johnny were catching all that had outdistanced them on the course. Into the forest trails, the Arabian kept up this advancing pace. Johnny marveled at the stamina of his mount. Then, up ahead, between some trees and around a bend, they caught sight of Matt and Dianna trailing just behind an appaloosa. The next time they were able to see them, Dianna was front of the spotted horse. Joshua picked up his speed, running yet faster.

They caught up to the app and went around it on the outside of a very sharp turn, Joshua's hindquarters circling behind his forehand. Matt and Dianna were still several lengths ahead. But as they came out of the woods and into the empty stretch of the last three-quarters of a mile, Joshua opened his mouth, drinking air, and edged closer to Dianna.

His nostrils flared by her flanks, then his eyes, his streaming mane. Now they were side by side, sprinting impossibly fast, sweating, eating up the ground.

The specter of tan tents surrounded with colors began to advance rapidly out of the distance. Both horses got another burst of speed and accelerated. Joshua was a little faster and went ahead of the mare by

almost half a length. Far up ahead, at the entrance to the maple grove, Johnny could see the huge crowd that had assembled. All the spectators at the start had had enough time to get there before the racing horses. Everyone was jumping up and down, waving and cheering.

Then Johnny realized that he and Joshua were in the lead. A supreme thrill of ecstasy overcame him and his mind could not function. He felt a rapturous joy. A memory as real and fresh as the reality of this moment remained with him always: The intense vision of hundreds of people wearing brightly colored shirts, dresses and sweaters, all bathed in the yellow light of the late autumn afternoon blended with the fluid, powerful, syncopated stride of his horse.

The trancelike quietness of this vision was suddenly shattered by a tremendous roar as the two roans pierced the center of the crowd, charging down the main avenue of the fairgrounds out of the big, round sun. Flying down the lane, through the grove of big maples which was filled with people, they crossed the finish line, the red roan leading the blue by just under half a length.

Johnny and Matt reined their horses to easy, quick halts and the crowd was swirling around them, both horses too exhausted for the moment to be mindful of the pressing mass of humans. They were steaming and lathered, breathing incredibly fast. Johnny and Matt were breathing fast too, but both of them were smiling.

Two officials began leading them through the cool grove back to the fairgrounds. Now other horses were galloping down the lane to the finish. There was cheering everywhere. Johnny was led into the winner's circle. Jacob, Sarah and Emily were waiting there. Ribbons were pinned to Joshua and Dianna's headstalls. The appaloosa was getting a ribbon too.

A large, colorful wreath of flowers was placed on Joshua's neck, and in the last, bright yellow rays of sunshine, a picture was made of the winning pair.

Part III

The Return

In the weeks following the Fair, Johnny began school. But he was able to continue living at home, now that he had a horse to ride. The first morning of school when he arrived riding Joshua, all the kids cheered. The camaraderie they felt then made going to school more appealing. Johnny Morgan was immediately popular. Everyone had great respect for him. In class, he was bright and attentive. He had plenty of help at home with his studies.

He enjoyed the long rides in the mornings and evenings. He loved the beauty. It thrilled him to see snow swirling off a peak for, in nature, the power of the wind impressed him most of all. And to him, that power was best revealed in blowing snow.

The hermit thrush and the meadowlark sang to him as he rode through the forest, and so did his favorite, the solitaire, sing to him its matchless song. Shep went along and waited outside all day, lying down near Joshua.

Johnny made lots of new friends.

About two weeks after the start of school, on the evening of the first heavy snowfall, Johnny came home with the news that the stock exchange in New York had collapsed.

"What?" asked Jacob. So Johnny explained all the details of the panic that he had learned of from his teacher.

"Well," said Jacob, "that needn't bother us up here." But there was a strange tone in his voice, and the family felt it. Johnny looked over at Matt and remembered what he had told him about harder times

that were foretold to come. But Matt wasn't looking at anyone and had nothing to say.

What Jacob had said was true enough. There was no need for this family to be affected very much by economic woes in New York, or the whole world for that matter. This farm provided everything it needed to sustain its own economy. It provided food, shelter, clothing, feed for the stock, and plenty of products to sell for cash at whatever the market price. Yet Jacob was affected. Though he liked not to think of it, he felt very much a part of his nation.

Every evening after dinner, Jacob asked his son for further news and Johnny had to enumerate all that he'd heard; about the worsening state of the economy, about people who were jumping out of buildings unable to face their lives minus their fortunes, and about something people were beginning to call a depression.

By the first of December, both Jacob and Sarah had solidly caught the mood of the times and Johnny wished he'd never said anything in the first place. After all, if he had not brought them the news, his parents wouldn't have heard about any of it yet.

But this was December first. This was the day he and his father always went together into the mountains to cut a Christmas tree.

Johnny forgot his moody thoughts and, in his excitement, popped out of his feathered-mattressed bed into the icy room, his bare feet clapping on the cold, wooden floor. He looked out his window. Well over two feet of snow had been in the valley since the end of October and a new coat of powder had covered everything during the night. But now the sky was completely clear. He watched the sun come up, spreading orange-yellow light across the white that was everywhere. Then he opened his window to smell and feel the outdoors and saw Joshua and Shep standing in the paddock down below, looking out into the distance, steam rising from their nostrils with each breath. Jacob and Matt had built another side onto the little shed and fixed up the inside to create a weather-tight, one horse stable. Joshua figured out how to operate the latch on the door and had gotten into the habit of opening it in the mornings so he and Shep could step outside.

Johnny dressed up and ran down the stairs and into the kitchen. Everyone else was already there. Breakfast was just being served, the hot biscuits and gravy being passed. He walked quickly into the room and slid into his place at the table. To his relief, everyone was in an especially happy mood.

"Hello, sleepyhead," Jacob said, running his fingers through his son's hair. "You must have had some good dreams last night. Did the sandman pay you a visit?" Johnny tucked his chin shyly. He liked it when his dad teased him that way.

Then his mother kissed his cheek. She held his face between her hands and smiled, gazing into his eyes. "Good morning Angel," she said softly.

'Mom always is making me feel wonderful,' he thought to himself and, realizing that for the first time, he appreciated her very much.

After a big breakfast of french toast with butter, maple syrup and sausage, Jacob, Johnny and Shep started across the deep snow with axe and saw. About nine o'clock they returned, got one of Jacob's plow horses and disappeared again into the white wilderness. In a little while, they came home. The horse was pulling a fifteen foot silver spruce. Never before had they taken such a large tree, but it would fit in the high-ceilinged parlour.

It took Matt and Jacob together to stand it in the tree stand. After lunch, the decorations were brought out and everyone began decorating the tree and making new ropes of popcorn, colored maize corn, and cranberries. A tall stepladder had to be brought in to decorate the top half of the tree. There were many kinds of ropes, many shapes and colors of glass bulbs, metal and wooden objects, candy canes, tinsel, candles with silver and gold reflectors, and a big blue and silver star on top which was lit by a candle inside it. Underneath, the Nativity was set up on a soft, white cotton material that surrounded the base of the tree. It was sunset before the pleasant work was finished. The tree had been set up before the fireplace with a couch placed to one side and three stuffed chairs on the other so that there was an open space in the middle warmed by the hearth. Outside, big snowflakes were drifting down.

After a candlelight dinner, Jacob, Sarah, Emily, Johnny, and Matt all sat in the parlour between the fire and the tree. The flames reflected on the tinsel and bulbs. It was a lovely sight and Jacob and Matt added to it by lighting all the candles on the tree. Matt read the story of the first Christmas from his Book. Then Sarah suggested they sing Christmas carols. They chose *We Three Kings* for their first one.

“Look,” Johnny exclaimed when they had finished. He was pointing at Emily. During the song, she had crawled under the tree and pulled a large, shiny gold bulb from the lowest branch. There she sat, the gold bulb in her lap. She was wearing a yellow-gold colored dress. There were golden curls hanging in ringlets all over her head, and the glow of the firelight upon her complexion was also of a golden hue.

The Spirit of Christmas had come.

December thirteenth dawned bright and sunny; a solid blue sky stretched over white mountains. On this day, the family made an annual Christmas visit to the village. It was the one night in the year that the family spent away from home. This year, though, Matt planned to return in the afternoon and watch over the farm.

Once again, Matt and Johnny rode their horses. Jacob took Sarah and Emily in the sleigh. It was painted bright red with yellow trim and had bells on the yoke, harness and reins. They jingled with each stride of the mare.

The travelers were dressed warm in coats of sheepskin with fleece lining, wool pants, fleece-lined leather gloves, and fur hats and boots. Inside the sleigh, there were finely tanned furs. Emily was tucked under a pile of them with only her face exposed and even that was covered much of the time with a hand loomed, woolen service blanket, colored in pastels with natural dyes.

The horses splashed through the trackless snow, extremely frisky in the cold air. They moved fast down one canyon and into the other. Though snow-encrusted trees were continuously passing overhead, Johnny had to squint his eyes to see into the glaring, white world.

Then, about halfway, a wind disturbed the crisp stillness, bringing clouds and then driving snow.

“This is a blizzard, Jake!” Matt had to yell to be heard. “We got to get shelter quick!”

“Let’s speed up, Matt. We’re almost there. If this gets any worse, we’re Lost!”

They trusted the horses to know the way and galloped them fast. By the time they reached the village the little group was enveloped in a blinding storm. They had to slow down and pick their way through the streets. Johnny and Matt rode close on either side of the black mare.

In the raging wind, Johnny could just hear Shep barking down beside Joshua but couldn't see him at all. Excepting Emily, each of them knew matter of factly that if they had been caught outside of town, they all might have perished.

The Conways had no idea of their arrival until they knocked on the door, though they had been watching for them.

"You poor, dear people. Get in here." Ruth had gotten distressed when the storm had first appeared.

"Mark, you and Dan get your coats on come with me," said Jeremy. "You folks get over by that fire. We'll tend to yer horses."

They all drank hot chocolate. Shortly afterward, Emily came down with a fever.

That afternoon the storm let up enough to see and Mark, Jeremy's oldest son, went for Dr. Parker in his father's sleigh.

When Johnny saw them returning, he got an idea.

"Matt, can we teach Joshua to pull the sleigh?"

"Sure, Matt said. "Come on."

Matt and Johnny went outside into the blowing snow. They carefully introduced Joshua to the harness, then hitched him up. Next, they unhitched him and led him around a little. They hitched him again and left him standing in the harness for about fifteen minutes. Then he was unhitched and stabled.

"You did fine," Matt complemented Joshua with a pat on the neck before they left him. "Tomorrow morning we'll hitch him up again and see if he'll pull."

As Matt and Johnny walked back into the house, the whistling blizzard increased again to blinding intensity. The snow blew through the house as they came in the door. Doctor Parker was looking at the label of a bottle through wire-rimmed glasses while speaking to Jacob and Sarah, his stethoscope hanging from his neck.

"She'll be all right if you keep her warm. It's just a cold. Babies get these hot fevers. Keep taking her temperature and give her lots of sage tea and half a teaspoon of this every four hours. Don't try to take her home until we get some good weather and her fever is gone. Call me if she isn't better in a day or two."

But the doctor had to wait over an hour before the storm lightened enough for him to go. Ruth, Sarah and some of the children

went shopping then, and Johnny went too. His first stop was McGurdy's Bootery, where he picked up a box already gift-wrapped.

That evening, the Christmas gifts were exchanged as was the custom of the two families. Everyone was deeply moved by Johnny's gift to Tommy while they watched him practice walking in his new orthopedic boots. The sole of the right one was raised. It was painful at first, but Tommy's joy overflowed as he walked for the first time in his life without a limp.

Then Johnny opened a gift. It was from Tommy: a hand-made leather collar for Shep. It was large, of heavy leather, and had big, silver rivets to protect Shep's neck. "Come're Shep," Johnny called from his place on the floor amidst wrapping paper and unopened packages. Shep trotted quickly to his side, and Johnny buckled on the new collar.

"Rear-rur-rur!" Shep called affectionately.

The still raging blizzard forced Matt to spend the night. All the children gathered around him and he told them stories from the Bible, but in his own words:

"So Moses became a sheepherder for Jethro, his father-in-law, way on the backside of the wilderness. He went out every day on his own. He liked his work and didn't want nobody to bother him.

"Well, one day when he was out, he happened to see a bush on fire. He went over to take a look because the bush wasn't bein' burned up by the fire at all. Then God spoke to him out of the bush.

" 'I am the God of your fathers, Abraham, Isaac, and Jacob. I have heard the cry of my people Israel who are in slavery and I have decided to set them free. Now take your sandals off 'cause this is Holy ground.'"

"He wanted Moses to go to the Pharaoh and tell him to let the Israelites go. But Moses had already had enough of the Israelites and the Pharaoh and told God to find somebody else.

"They argued about it for a while, but God finally got mad and tole Moses to get goin'.

"So Moses walked all the way back to Egypt. He was eighty years old by then, but he was strong from workin' outside so much.

"When he got to Pharaoh and told him that God said to let the Israelites go, the Pharaoh thought he was crazy.

"When he started talkin' to the Israelites about leavin' Egypt, they got scared and changed their minds, 'specially when the Pharaoh started

makin' things hot for 'em. He did that because Moses was doin' all kinds of miracles, one after the other, as God showed him, which were hurtin' the Egyptians pretty bad.

"Finally, after the Passover, Pharaoh gave up and let 'em go."

What kind of miracles did Moses do?" asked Ralph.

"Oh, he turned their water into blood, he brought frogs, lice, flies an' hail as big as watermelons to the land. 'Course, none of this happened to the Israelites. Then all the Egyptians got boils," replied Matt.

"How come God was doin' all this mean stuff to those poor people when the Israelites didn't even want to go?" asked Judy.

"Well, really, the Egyptians had been meaner to the Israelites over the years than God was to the Egyptians. But this story shows that God always carries out his plans no matter what people say or do."

"Why?" asked Mark.

"Cause God made people to be free. He hates slavery an' He knows that people have slavery and other problems because they're too greedy an' cowardly. He wants us to be generous and courageous. We can, too, each one of us. But God will go ahead and carry out His plans even if no one is willing to help Him. Otherwise, nothin' would ever make any sense."

"Well, how come God was so nice to Moses?" asked Judy. "Seems to me Moses wasn't always too perfect neither."

"No, honey, he wasn't always perfect. He was a great man an' he was the humblest man who ever lived, but still, he was a man, like other men. An' really, God is good to everybody."

"Ya, okay, but how come He helped Moses so much?" Judy persisted.

"Well, there's just one reason for that," Matt replied. "Moses liked God. He was His friend."

There were only three rooms in the Conway house. Although they had seven children, Jeremy and Ruth slept cozily together with all of them in one bedroom. The Morgans, with Matt, slept in the parlour. The house stayed warm all night, though the temperature outside dropped to thirty-five below.

At sunrise the sky was clear, and Emily's fever had broken. After

breakfast, Matt and Johnny went out and harnessed Joshua to the sleigh again. Johnny sat in the sleigh and took the reins while Matt asked the graceful equine to walk. At first, Joshua wouldn't pull the strange weight behind him. He went sideways, then tried to back up—any direction but forward. But Matt and Johnny urged him calmly, smiling at the speckled animals antics. Finally he jerked the sleigh a couple of times. And then he started to pull. In a while, Matt was leading him as Joshua pranced smartly up and down the street.

It suddenly occurred to Matt that he had been glancing instinctively over his shoulder and observing a squall moving in from the west. He let Johnny take over and went into the house to talk with Jacob.

"You'd better stay another day," Jacob warned.

"No, Jake, I'm gonna go. I'll take what I need to survive in case Dianna and me get caught in a storm. I'm comin' back down the first morning it looks good so I can accompany you back home."

Matt went out to the stable, got Dianna ready and headed out. He waved to Johnny and then cantered out of town.

In time, Johnny and his horse got pretty skilled at driving the sleigh

Mark had been watching them through the a window going up and down the street. He watched the horse change from walk to trot to canter and then back down through the gaits at the child's commands.

And he watched them as, a couple of times, Joshua got fed up with the learning and started bouncing on his forehand, his ears thrown back. When that happened, he saw Johnny relax completely and sit quietly in the sleigh, looking around. In a while, he started talking to his stallion, laughing at his own stories. Eventually Joshua began to move forward again on his own, and then Johnny took control so lightly that the horse never noticed.

"Dad," Mark asked finally, "can I hitch Mertle to the sleigh and go for a drive with Johnny?"

Jeremy scratched his head for a moment. "I guess so. Why don't you take the kids with you?"

This brought a lot of happy excitement into the house, which was quickly carried outside with the children. They hitched their dappled mare to the sleigh and Johnny was enjoined in the street. All the Conway children couldn't fit in one sleigh, so some of them rode with Johnny.

Then their friends who lived nearby began to appear and started taking turns riding around the village in the two sleighs.

That afternoon, Johnny happened to see Robert who, though older than Johnny, was one of his best friends at school. He waved to him from his sleigh, but Robert did not wave back. Instead, he turned and ran out of sight around the corner. In half an hour, he reappeared driving a sleigh pulled by a very handsome black and white paint. Now there were three sleighs racing around the snow-filled village, all packed with happy passengers. Then the snowfall got heavy again. Everyonc was forced to give up the fun.

"Look!" Robert exclaimed as they were about to separate, "let's get back together and keep going as soon as we can."

"Yeah!" said Johnny, and all the children said, "Yeah!"

Back inside the Conway's warm little house, Johnny felt the contrast between happy, rosy-cheeked children and somber adults. He had noticed that Jeremy and Ruth didn't seem their usual selves the day before. Now the reason became apparent. With the inclement weather, the adults found nothing better to do than sit inside and listen to the radio. Depressing news had already taken a toll on his aunt and uncle. Now his mom and dad, hearing the morbid broadcasts and talking to their worried friends, were succumbing to the mood, and their cheer slowly faded. He watched it all happen while he watched the snow pile up outside.

The other children could not have been more oblivious to all this. When the blizzard lifted toward sunset, they asked excitedly if they could hitch up the sleighs again and their parents nodded their approval. Once out into the cold air, Johnny forgot completely what was happening indoors. He hitched Joshua to the sleigh and was off... Tommy always rode beside him. The two sleighs went past Robert's house, and in a short while he cantered up beside them. Then Pate, another of Johnny's friends, appeared in his parents' sleigh. Twilight disappeared, but there was the moon and light cast from gas lamps. So the children kept up their play until the snow thickened once more.

Joshua and Mertle were unhitched, rubbed down and fed. Johnny and his seven cousins all worked together in coordinated effort.

Johnny was the last child to come in the door of the little house.

He noticed immediately that Emily had developed a cough. Also, some friends were visiting.

Amarante and the beautiful Ophelia Espinoza were locked in conversation with Jacob and Sarah and Jeremy and Ruth. Amarante, Jeremy, and Jacob had all served together in France.

"Ola, patroncito!" exclaimed a large, ruggedly handsome, black-mustached man as soon as his eyes caught sight of Johnny. "Come, quate, sit here!"

Johnny matched Amarate's smile and excitement with his own as he bounded spritely onto the man's lap.

"Ooh, you know," Amarante told him, "that I am going to take another vacation next summer so we can stay camped out together again?"

The news made Johnny so happy that he pressed the side of his small face tightly against the man's cheek, hugging him with his little arms tightly around Amarante's neck.

Amarante had taken a "vacation" in the summer of twenty-eight after he found out about Johnny herding his father's flocks by himself. The two of them spent three weeks in the wilderness, trailing the sheep together.

During this experience, Johnny had learned in great detail the art of the shepherd.

"You have a big responsibility," Amarante had explained to him over and over again. "Always remember that you are in charge here. You must feel that way and know that it is so. Then you will succeed." That was why Amarante always called Johnny "patroncito".

The man also showed the child ways to catch elusive cutthroats, and they spent hours together watching and tracking wild animals, studying their habits, while, at the same time, gathering native herbs for food, seasoning and medicine.

"Tommy will be there, too. He's going to stay the summer with us so we can trail the sheep together," Johnny said.

"That is very, very good!" Amarante replied. "The three of us will have a tremendously good time together."

The man unbuttoned and removed Johnny's coat, shook off

the melting snow, and laid it on the floor next to the couch. Then he continued with his conversation.

"I do not know," Amarante was saying. "I have not sold many caballos since this stock market has crashed. I will have to buy more feed in the spring."

"I can give you lots of hay. I'll never use up all the hay I've got stacked. I can give you grain, too," Jacob offered.

"Gracias, amigo, that may be a lifesaver, but my business must pay for itself if it is going to survive."

"Well, you can always move to yer father's ranch down on the Gallinas if you have to," suggested Jeremy. "With all his pasture, you're bound to be all right."

"Oh, sure, but that would be very depressing for us, really," Amarante replied. "We love living here."

"Yes," Ophelia put in. "We are very happy here. It would never be the same again if we have to leave. And Pate' and Tina are doing so well in school."

"And, besides," Amarante explained, "I could lease pasture around here if I have to. But I can't sell horses off a big pasture. I have to have horses clean in their own stalls for the public to appreciate them and pay a fair price."

"Too bad everyone invested so much in the stock market. No one has any money to spend now. They're laying off at the mill. Some say it might close altogether." Jeremy was distraught, and due to heavy snow, no one could work. He wouldn't be drawing a paycheck this week.

"I'm still shocked at how fast my investments disappeared," he went on. "I know I told you already, Jacob, but I want to say it again; I am sorry I lost your money."

"Forget it, pal. Everybody lost their money. We're all in this together." But everyone knew that Jacob and Sarah were about the only people around who were not caught up in economic hardship.

Ophelia was holding Sarah's baby. Emily began to cough spasmodically. Ophelia put the baby on her shoulder and patted her back, but it didn't help so she passed the child back to Sarah who was able, finally, to quiet her.

Hearing the water boil, Ruth got up and went into the kitchen. She returned with tea and cookies.

'Well, its Christmas time." Jeremy didn't want to be a poor host. "Let's see, eight o'clock, Amarante the radio, please."

Amarante was sitting closest to the shiny, wooden box. He put his fingers on the knob and it clicked. There was a squack, then the stern voice of a newsman.

"And now the news, President Hoover blamed Congress today for the nosedive plunge in corporate stock prices last October. Meanwhile, sales volumes continue to decline in many industries and several firms closed their doors today..."

"Hey," Jeremy broke in. "What's going on? That's supposed to be the Radio City Christmas Program."

When the guests left for home, it was bedtime. All the kids decided to sleep together in the kitchen. About five a.m., one of them, Ralph, woke up and noticed that it had stopped snowing. He woke the others. Very quietly, all the children got dressed and stepped out into the freezing air. They harnessed the horses by lamplight.

The perfect silence was disturbed only by the two sleighs. None of the children spoke, being enthralled in the mystery surrounding them. There was no moon now. The only light to drive by was from the street lamps. Snow crystals sparkled with color like scattered gems. Then, as paled light filtered through the clouds, other sleighs joined them in the streets. When the blizzard descended on them around nine in the morning, there were six sleighs full of children dashing through the village. Johnny and his cousins walked in, wondering what kind of trouble they were up to their ears in. But their parents only half-heartedly asked when they had left the house. That was all! From then on, the children never bothered to ask if they could go out. They just watched from the kitchen window, and whenever the storm let up enough to give them visibility, day or night, they went out sleighing. In between, they spent their time sleeping, eating, and playing games. Johnny got to know his cousins well. There was Mark, Dan, Carol, Ralph, Linda, Judy, Tommy, and Kevin, in order of age. The intermittent blizzard kept up. No one could work or go to school. There were enough children borrowing their father's sleighs that every child in the village was able to take part in the fun. The snow depth was now well over four feet.

Johnny was keenly aware of his sister's rasping cough. He spent much of his time holding her when he was inside. He worried about

her and about his parents. Their dispositions had completely fallen into darkness, worse than in the previous months. They just sat around all the time looking very glum.

But as soon as he was outside, driving Joshua along, Johnny's worries disappeared. There was only sheer happiness then. Often the children raced their horse-drawn sleds, but none of them could beat Joshua, not once, no matter how many children were packed into Johnny's sleigh. Some of the other sleighs were pulled by teams, but Joshua outran all of them. Johnny was careful though. He would not allow his Arabian to become overly tired and walked him most of the time.

It went on for a whole week like that. Then, late one night, the children went out under a moonlit sky at midnight. They stayed out all night. The moon went down. In a few hours, the sun rose. The jingling sleighs could be heard all morning. By eleven o'clock, everyone was near the center of town. The sleighs began racing up and down Main Street. The children were throwing snowballs at each other as they passed. It was good-natured fun, though, and no one was seriously hurt. A few of the smaller ones cried a little when they were hit in the face.

Adults began gathering along the sidewalks to watch the children. Shopkeepers came out of their shops to watch and talk with their neighbors. By mid-afternoon most of the village had gathered along Main Street, a great crowd. And they weren't talking about the sad state of the nation, but about their children all playing together before them and about other matters of purely local interest. People were smiling. Christmas was approaching. The sky was cloudy and threatening, but the villagers found that they had a lot to be happy about. They were out in the cold, sobering air. When it got too cold standing around, they could go into one of the shops or stores for a while, then come back outside and watch their children and grandchildren driving their parents' sleighs back and forth, throwing thousands of snowballs, racing, laughing. Johnny noticed his parents and his aunt and uncle out at various times. He knew that someone always remained at home with Emily. Once, Jacob threw a snowball at him when Johnny trotted by and hit him on the side of the head. The next time he went by, Johnny threw one back at his father who was talking to someone. It hit his neck and snow slid down his back. Jacob turned and shook his fist, but he was laughing and thoroughly pleased with his son's accuracy from the moving sled.

About eight p.m., a cold wind came up and everyone seemed to disappear at once. The children went home, ate a big dinner, then fell asleep immediately.

Johnny awoke to the sound of Matt and Jacob talking. The sky was clear and bright. It was nearly ten o'clock. Although Matt was still warming himself by the stove after his long ride, it was decided they should leave at once. Within ten minutes, Johnny was dressed and outside and saddling Joshua.

The great quantity of snow made it hard for the black mare to pull the sleigh after leaving the village streets. It was uphill all the way home. Once inside the big canyon, the sunshine gave way to dense fog as the little party of travelers climbed into a cloud. The horses' legs sank into snow way past their knees and hock joints, and visibility was only about twenty feet. Just the edges of things loomed past along the trail. Then a cold wind came up, blowing down the canyon into their faces. They turned up the canyon leading to their farm. Big snowflakes were swirling in the wind. The fog had blown away but the sun didn't return. The black mare was very tired now, making painfully slow progress, fighting the wind, the snow and the heavy sleigh.

"Let's switch horses," Matt yelled his loudest to be heard amidst the wind's violence. The men jumped into the deepening snow and fumbled at the harness with numb fingers. They unhitched the mare, replacing her with Joshua. Johnny's teeth were chattering uncontrollably. (He didn't care. The chickadees were singing and playing on the tree trunks and the blowing snow thrilled him.) He was forced to ride in the sleigh under the furs. But Joshua leapt away with the heavy sled as though the snow did not bother him at all. Matt ponied the black mare. The canyon spread out into their valley. The log house came into view, and they were home.

As soon as everyone was inside, the storm closed in upon them. All that could be seen without was whiteness. The log house was icy cold. All the fires were lit, but the temperature outside continued to drop and the big house wouldn't warm up. Emily's fever returned. Her coughing grew deeper and thicker, rattling her little frame. The blizzard raged for two days and nights, and though they kept her wrapped up and close to the big stove in the bedroom, Emily got worse. The tightening congestion made her breathing labored and weak.

Strangely, Johnny could not worry. Now that this dreaded day had arrived, he was not panicked at all. No, on the contrary, he was growing calmer by the moment. Jacob and Sarah were getting frantic with fear, but Johnny could only watch it all. 'Maybe after worrying about this for so long, there's no more left in me,' he thought. Then he realized that it was the other part of the vision, Emily's healing, that was intriguing him. He even wanted to worry for his little sister, but he couldn't because he was expecting something to happen.

On the morning of the third day after arriving home, on Christmas Eve, Johnny arose at the very crack of dawn. Outside, there was a dense ice fog. He got dressed and went out, practically swimming through the snow just to reach Joshua's paddock. He opened the door of the little stable, and Joshua and Shep walked out. The ice fog started glittering brightly as the sun rose. They could only see ten or fifteen feet into the fog. It lasted until mid-morning. When it lifted, the sky was clear and everything was covered with a thick glaze of ice. It was exceedingly beautiful. Finally, the child went into the house.

Jacob and Matt were standing in the kitchen between cookstove and the breakfast table, but no breakfast was being prepared.

"She's slippin', Matt. She's slippin' fast. I don't know where to turn. We shoulda stayed at Jeremy and Ruth's. I really feel lost. Nowhere to turn."

Matt's response contrasted with Jacob's panic; it was measured and slow.

"Calm yourself, Jake. Do that first. Healing can only come when there ain't no tension at all. Then go stick close to Emily and Sarah. I'll ski down the mountain, straight to Doc Parker's. He can advise me and give me medicines, then I'll come back on snowshoes. I'll get back just as quick as I can."

As Matt was walking out, he stopped to look at Johnny. Their eyes caught for a moment. Then Matt was gone.

Wearily, Jacob walked out of the kitchen and up the stairs. Neither he nor Sarah had been able to sleep. Jacob had taken up biting his nails, something Johnny had never seen him do before. Some of his fingernails were actually bleeding. Sarah had nervously rubbed her right cheek until it was raw, the skin broken. Blood trickled down her face.

The boy did not join his family upstairs but sat down by the

fireplace instead. He spent the morning feeding wood into the fire and watching the flames. A little before noon, he saw bright colors appearing on the hearth, emerging out of the firelight. The slanting rays of the late December sun had transported the colored shapes of the stained glass window into the center of the parlour. Johnny watched as the beautiful image moved ever so slowly across the floor, away from the fire, toward the Christmas tree, while the sun migrated from the late morning, to noon, to early afternoon. When it came to a point almost under the tree, the image faded and disappeared.

It began to snow very hard again, and Johnny knew that Matt would not be able to return today.

At twilight, Jacob and Sarah came out of their room and walked slowly down the stairs. Sarah was holding the still form of Emily in her arms. Jacob began lighting the lamps while Sarah went over and stood in front of the fireplace, between the hearth and the Christmas tree. Jacob got the stepladder and lit all the candles on the big tree. Then he went to stand next to Sarah.

Johnny laid down on the floor. He placed his head on the exact spot where the colored image had disappeared. From here, he could look up and see the full height of the tree towering above him, the ornaments shining in the firelight. He could hear Emily's shallow, rasping breaths. Occasionally Jacob banked the big fire. Except for that, no one moved for many hours.

As Johnny lay there, looking up at the tree, only one thought would come into his mind. That thought kept returning. It was something Matt had told him that evening when he'd first come: "You'll know what to do. The Spirit will show you."

As time passed, Johnny became aware that he was going to do something, that the Spirit would show him what it would be, and that he was waiting there to be shown.

The child was completely at peace, exactly the way he had been with his friend in the cave. And he realized that his friend really was there with him, watching over him, like he'd said.

At that moment, Jacob spoke, "Oh God, I haven't even thought to pray. I don't even know how to pray. Oh God, please save Emily." Sarah began to cry. Johnny looked over at his parents. It was exactly what he'd

seen in the flames. His vision was now a reality before his eyes.

Suddenly he knew what to do. He sprang to his feet and ran to the kitchen where he donned his sheepskin coat, his overpants, mittens, and his overboots and fur hat. Then he opened the door and entered the freezing blast outside. He could not see more than a few feet through the blizzard, though the bright moonlight illuminated the white world like the inside of a lampglobe. He felt his way around the house, pushing through the deep snow. He was already exhausted as he reached for the latch on the door to Joshua's little stable. But when he stepped inside, his horse nickered to him. The greeting gave him a new burst of strength, and the boy started tacking him up quickly. He opened the door again and rode out into the raging, windswept night.

Joshua went slowly, with great difficulty. He sank down past his girth into the snow. Johnny relied on him to know the way through the blinding storm. Shep made his way alongside by jumping and swimming through the white sea.

At the sheep pen, Johnny stopped his mount for a brief rest and peered over the high plank fence. Inside were clustered roundish piles of white snow, each pile representing a sheep. Johnny knew they were warm inside their snow covering, thanks to their thick coats of curling fleece. 'There will be a lot of wool this spring,' he thought.

They continued on through the pasture, and the wind began to die down, the snowfall lightened up. By the time they reached the steep slope between the jagged pinnacles, it had become perfectly still and stopped snowing. Through the clouds, the full moon lit up everything with an intense glow. As far as Johnny looked, he could see the details of things because the snow reflected the diffuse moonlight. The whole world was bright like daytime, and it was near midnight. The child looked back at his home. He could even see the smoke curling out of the fireplace chimney.

"Come on" he urged and Joshua started up the invisible trail. The horse advanced by leaps, one at a time. Slowly, steadily, they ascended, up and up. Joshua was breathing fast and had to take frequent rests between his series of upward leaps. Then, perhaps thirty feet below their destination, their route steepened slightly, and the agile equine could make no more progress. Though he leapt with all his strength, his body wouldn't move from its place. He was buried so that only his neck and head were out of the snow. The saddle had disappeared. Johnny was holding onto his mane with nothing but the disturbed surface of the snow under his outstretched body. Still, Joshua continued leaping upward, but the boy halted him because he was only burying himself deeper. Johnny began to crawl. He went about eight feet more, but after that, he was only digging a hole, getting no farther, and burying his horse in the process. All the boy could see of him was the delicately formed head above the pile of snow he'd created between them.

"Now what do we do," he said aloud.

Then, in the bright stillness of the night, there was heard the loud howling of a wolf pack, and they were not far off. Joshua and Shep both pricked up their ears. Shep sniffed the air cautiously. Joshua snorted quietly, taking in slow breaths through widely flaring nostrils, examining the air. His eyes were big and round, but he did not turn and run away. Johnny stiffened suddenly and felt a surge of adrenaline through his body. It seemed his quest was over.

Then he remembered the wolf he'd seen the last day he'd taken out his sheep. He smiled. The wolf gave him an idea.

"Shep." Shep made his way over to his master. The boy wrapped his arm around the dog's body, hooking his fingers inside the big, leather collar. The dog began leaping up the slope. Though Johnny's weight held him back considerably, he was able to drag the boy up through the snow, swimming toward the hollow tree. At last, Johnny got a hand on the old trunk and pulled himself up to it. He had to dig deep in the snow before finding the hole into which he'd placed his flute months ago. He took off the big mittens to fit his hand inside. But the bees had filled the hole with propolis, and it was frozen hard. The shepherd reached his hand back to his knife and removed it from its sheath. He began stabbing it into the propolis until he'd hacked out a hole large enough for his hand. Inside, it was nice and warm. He moved his fingers to loosen them from their numbness. Then he got hold of the flute and pulled it out. He held it up and smiled, though the muscles and skin of his face, burning with cold, did not move. It glistened in the moonlight.

The wolves were still howling as Johnny crawled and rolled easily down the steep incline to his horse, and then he wheeled him around. Joshua accomplished this maneuver by rearing three times in succession, pulling his front legs out of the deep snow while pivoting his hind legs with great power, for they were deeply buried. With the three successive rearing leaps, the stallion made the one hundred and eighty degree swing and then leaped down the snowy mountain. In less than a minute, they were all the way down and into the valley. Now the going was hard again as the horse pushed through the shallow rut he'd left coming up. A biting wind arose and Johnny's hands, face, legs, and feet became numb. But he held on to the precious flute and stoically endured the slow journey back.

When they got into the protection of the small stable, Johnny slid from the saddle and nearly collapsed as his legs, having no sensation at all, buckled under the impact of the landing. But feeling began pulsing back into them, first numbness, and then pain. His delicate hands pulled the saddle and bridle off his exhausted mount and put some oats in the manger. "I'll be back," he called going out, and closed the door behind him.

He made his way painfully around the house, through the deep snow and cold wind, finally entering through the back door. He took off his coat, hat, overpants, mittens and boots and walked into the parlour.

Jacob and Sarah were still standing in the little warm space between the fireplace and the bright, shining Christmas tree. Sarah was holding the dying Emily. They both were looking at her with haggard faces. Sarah was crying. Everything looked exactly the same as it did before Johnny went out. They hadn't noticed him leave, and didn't notice him return, so absorbed were they by grief and by the fleeting life of the baby.

Johnny's hands, face and feet were still quite numb. He stood there watching his family, unnoticed. He began to cry. Silent tears flowed down his cheeks in the soft glow of the firelight. He stood there for a long time until his body found its warmth again. Then, carefully, he put his crystal flute to his mouth and began to play.

All the notes of the beautiful melody came out perfectly, and the flute lit up immediately. A light shined upon his mother, father and baby sister, glowing warmly on their skin. It made them look fresh, young, alive. The pallor in Emily's face disappeared. She smiled, then opened her eyes. The faces of his parents became bright with renewed life. Their eyes opened wide with wonder as they looked down at their baby who was smiling up at them. Then they all looked at Johnny. Not only was the flute glowing, but his whole body became a temple of bright, living light.

Down in the little stable, the horse pricked his ears and stopped

munching his hay in mid-bite to listen to the familiar melody coming distinctly on the winter wind. The dog listened, too, lying in his warm bed of straw, panting contentedly. He tilted up his head, touching the paw of a kitten with his nose. The kitten, standing above him on the manger, wanted to play.

Readers Guide

1. Why did Johnny herd the sheep deep into the wilderness instead of just to the top of the valley above their farm as his father intended.

2. Why did Johnny leave his sheep in a high mountain valley in order to follow a man he had never met before?

3. How did Johnny's father and mother react to his story about how he acquired the horse while out herding the sheep?

4. When did Johnny begin to become concerned about Emily?

5. How would you describe the relationship between Johnny's parents: Jacob and Sarah?

6. Why did Johnny's mother, Sarah, stop worrying about Johnny being out alone in the wilderness for so long herding the family's sheep herd?

7. Johnny's relationship with his cousin Tommy was very special. How did Tommy benefit from his relationship with Johnny?

8. Why did Jacob decide to hire his old friend Matt Slade to work on the family's farm?

9. Matt was a horse trainer. Did Matt believe Johnny's story about how he acquired his horse, Joshua?

10. How did Matt's story about his wife, Rachael, relate to Johnny's sister, Emily?

11. What was the first thing that Matt instructed Johnny to do to begin the training of his horse Joshua?

12. What did Matt have to say about Johnny that convinced his mother, Sarah, to allow Johnny to enter the annual cross-country race?

13. How did Johnny react to the wolf that was watching him herd his flock into the wilderness for the last time during the year, when the aspen leaves had become gold streaked with red?

14. What was Johnny's Christmas gift to Tommy, that he purchased with money his father paid him for herding the sheep, and how did that gift affect Tommy's life?

15. What inspired Johnny to get his dog, Shep, to enable him to continue uphill through the deep snow so that he could retrieve his flute?

www.ingramcontent.com/pod-product-compliance
Lightning Source LLC
Chambersburg PA
CBHW010357310726
48979CB00006B/1070
* 9 7 8 1 6 3 2 9 3 5 7 9 3 *